SAVE YOUR
HEART FOR ME

SAVE YOUR HEART FOR ME

•

Joye Ames

AVALON BOOKS
NEW YORK

Published by Thomas Bouregy & Co., Inc.
160 Madison Avenue, New York, NY 10016

PRINTED IN THE UNITED STATES OF AMERICA
ON ACID-FREE PAPER
BY HADDON CRAFTSMEN, BLOOMSBURG, PENNSYLVANIA

Chapter One

"Carson? Is that you?" The Union captain put away his ornamental sword and pushed back his hat. "Don't you know me?"

Carson blinked her eyes and tried to focus. The crowd was very still around them and the moment seemed to stretch out forever.

From behind her, Lauren cleared her throat, and Carson shook her head.

"That *is* you, isn't it?" he guessed. His eyes raked her face and there was no doubt. "Carson Myszkowski!"

"I can't believe it," Carson finally responded, recognizing his face. "Alex?"

"What are you doing?" Lauren hissed. "People are watching! You can do old home week later!"

"Sorry." Alex pulled at his large cavalry gloves as he recalled where they were and what they were supposed to be doing. It was just such a surprise to see Carson there.

Carson glanced at the crowd, seeing her parents' faces and pulled herself together. It was just such a surprise to see Alex there.

"Mrs. Anne Butcher," Alex addressed Carson in a formal voice loud enough to be heard above the murmurings of the crowd at the gates.

Carson stared at him, forgetting her lines for a moment while her mind raced with memories and questions. She didn't move, didn't speak while the crowd grew restive, starting to whisper.

" *'Yes, I am Anne Butcher! Yes, I am Anne Butcher!'* " a voice from behind her prompted her lines.

"Yes." It came out barely audible in the large open space, with a cow lowing from the barn and the far sound of geese overhead. She cleared her throat and adjusted her voice a little louder. "Yes, I am Anne Butcher."

The crowd relaxed as though the world had swung into its proper axis again. Carson's parents hugged each other.

"I am Captain Michael Payne of the U.S. Army under General Sherman," Alex continued. "You will surrender this farm to me."

"Please," she pleaded, hoping the tone was eloquent. "Please don't destroy my home. I have worked so hard to keep us going since my husband's death."

Captain Michael Payne smiled at her but his tone was firm. "It has been my judgment to use this farm and this house as a base hospital for the wounded of both our sides, Mrs. Butcher. The horses and the livestock will be confiscated by my troops to refresh our own needs. But the house will not be damaged."

Carson stood looking up at him for a few seconds

too long, and she heard Mrs. Engstrom hiss, "Swoon! Swoon!"

Captain Michael Payne's golden eyes twinkled at her. His left brow raised slightly as he waited for the end of the tableau.

It was his daring look. The way he'd always looked at her when he wanted her to do something stupid when they were kids. The look that always worked because she didn't want him to think that she was chicken.

"Thank heaven!" she finally managed. She bent her knees as she had practiced, and closed her eyes, relying on the "captain" to catch her in his arms and not let her drop to the ground.

His gloved hands slid around her waist and held her then, he looked back at his men.

"No one here is to be harmed. Any trespassers will answer to me personally. Gather up the wounded from the camp and bring them here. The battle of Butcher's Roost is over."

Applause sounded through the large group of watchers around the house and yard. The men in uniform began to pick themselves up and brush themselves off, finding hats and weapons that had been dropped during the fake assault.

Carson opened her eyes and looked up at the captain, struggling to get her footing so that she didn't fall on the ground when he released her.

"I thought you weren't going to swoon!" Mrs. Engstrom came down the stairs, clutching her hand to her throat. "For one awful minute, I thought you weren't going to swoon! You took a year off of my life, Carson! What were you thinking?"

"Sorry, Mrs. Engstrom," Carson replied quietly. "I guess it was stage fright."

Mrs. Engstrom sighed and mentally crossed Carson Myszkowski off of her play list for next year.

"I thought it was masterful timing," Alex whispered, helping Carson stand up straight.

"Thanks." She brushed at her dress. "It was more a dread fear that you might forget to catch me. You know how easy I am to *forget*."

Alex frowned. "I never forgot you, Carson."

"Five years!" She rounded on him as the yard around them cleared. "And only a handful of letters! Then you're back and you didn't even tell me!"

"Hey, you were pretty good, Carson!" Her brother approached, his uniform torn in several places. "But I thought you weren't going to swoon for a minute." He put out his hand to Alex. "Good fight, Captain."

"Thanks, Private."

Riley Myszkowski studied the other man's face for an instant. "Hey, Alex! Is that you? What are you doing here? When did you get back?"

"I moved back last week, Riley. I haven't had time to call everyone," Alex said, looking into Carson's eyes as though to answer her accusation.

"It's been a while! I think you owe me a pizza!" Riley recalled with a quick laugh. "And maybe ten bucks! I'll be looking for you, Captain."

"Maybe the pizza, Riley," Alex answered. "I can't believe you're still trying to scrounge money off of everyone!"

Riley shrugged. "Not everything changes."

"Hello!" Lauren sailed down the porch steps and situated herself between both men with a dazzling smile. "Why, the two of you must be so thirsty after your ordeal!" Her "Scarlett" accent was never better. She'd played Anne Butcher for the previous two years. "Let me take you around back for some lemonade."

She put a hand through each of the men's arms and the group walked away. Both men smiled down into her pretty, upturned face.

Carson started to follow but a small boy, not more than five, came up to her and pulled at her dress.

"Hey, lady?"

Lauren glanced back at her and made a discouraging face then continued walking and talking with her escorts.

Carson narrowed her eyes and picked up the hem of her dress, prepared to follow no matter what Lauren had in mind.

"Hey! Lady!" the child called in a louder voice.

His parents joined him and looked at Carson, waiting for her to acknowledge their son.

Carson ground her teeth as Lauren, Riley, and Alex rounded the corner of the house.

"Yes?" she asked with a sigh, trying to be pleasant.

"Are you a witch?"

It took a while to explain to the small boy, whose name was Thomas, that she wasn't a witch but a widow. Then to explain what a widow did and why she wore black. By the time she'd finished, Mrs. Engstrom was drawing her into the house to answer questions for a crowd of visitors that were taking the tour of the pre-Civil War farmhouse.

Carson glanced out the wide, narrow-paned window and saw Lauren flirting with both her brother and Alex Langston. She didn't care if she flirted with Riley. He was used to it. She didn't *really* care if she flirted with Alex, but she did have a few choice words to say to him and the sooner she said them, the sooner she'd feel better about it.

Alex was back. She couldn't believe it! And she couldn't believe that she was still angry at his desertion. It had been five years, after all. She wasn't normally a person to hold a grudge. Alex was a different story.

There was no time to go and look for Alex, Riley, and Lauren. She had no sooner finished with the tour than she was "summoned" for assignment in the field.

"Ladies!" Mrs. Engstrom called frantically from the porch again.

Twice every year the small town of Seven Springs, Tennessee came alive. Once in the fall for the apple festival and just after Christmas for the reenactment and craft fair at the resident historical site.

Butcher's Roost had been preserved since the end of the Civil War as a reminder of the great battle between the North and the South. Resting on several hundred acres of land at the foot of the great Smoky Mountains, it had been a strategic site for one of the last headquarters of the Confederate army.

Despite its unattractive name, the house and land were graceful and well made, weathering time and tourist's feet with a dignity that had been built into its foundation.

Mrs. Engstrom, the last descendent of the liaison between Confederate landowner Anne Butcher and Union officer Michael Payne, was in charge of the event, as always. She handed out assignments with the deliberate strength of a general commanding her troops. She knew every word of every line that was spoken during the play. If a rifle misfired during the assault, she caught her breath. She was the original

Mrs. Anne Butcher for the first ten years of the tableau. She gave way only when she became unable to fit in the dress.

"Jean, you will be handling the tours through the house until noon." She checked off her list without looking up, her bifocals perched on the end of her nose.

"Melanie, you'll be taking the groups through the spinning and dye house. I have Tom taking people through the servants' quarters and the smokehouse."

Melanie made a face but smiled as the woman looked up at her.

"Is that a problem, dear?"

"Not at all, Mrs. Engstrom."

Everyone knew her reputation. If she checked you off the list, you would never be part of the reenactment again.

Mrs. Engstrom glared at Melanie but didn't comment. She continued on with her list and everyone breathed a sigh of relief.

"Lauren, you'll be working at the souvenir shop, taking money and setting up the tours. Mind you." She pointed her pencil at her. "No more than ten or twelve at a time. We don't want to lose track of any of them like we did last year and end up with someone locked in the cellar, do we?"

Melanie nudged Lauren and laughed. Lauren had lost an entire tour last year, and obviously the chairperson of the Seven Springs Historical Society wasn't going to trust her in the house again.

"And Carson, since you're new, you'll be doing storytelling beside Mary, who's candle-dipping, and Rachel, who's making soap."

Carson nodded and thanked her, silently wondering

exactly how long it took in Seven Springs to become an insider.

She'd been an outsider since she'd moved there in her last year of high school. Five years later, she was still "someone new."

She trudged back up the steep slope to the demonstration area near the barn and outbuildings, trying not to think about that awful first year in Seven Springs.

Things had been so much better since she'd come back from college and made a life for herself in the town. She'd found friends and been accepted by most people.

She'd joined the Historical Society while she'd still been in college, studying to be a history teacher. It was a good place to meet people and her natural love of history made it interesting. But from the first, she'd suffered the fate of the last man on the bottom.

The first year, she'd been making soap. The second, she'd been dipping candles. Last year, she'd been out in the stables answering questions about the chickens and cattle.

Thank heavens three other "outsiders" had moved into town and joined up for the reenactment after her. At least storytelling didn't smell bad or entail her having animals stepping on her feet.

The storytelling stall was the one next to the blacksmith. There was a chair crudely made of slats and rope and several smaller stools surrounding it for the storyteller and her patient listeners. Everything had to be authentic, something that could have been created during the Civil War. Mrs. Engstrom and the Historical Society were scrupulous when it came to realism.

By the time Carson got to her spot, some parents

had already dropped off a few solemn-looking little children who were patiently waiting for the story of the battle of Butcher's Roost. Many of them were dressed as their parents had imagined children dressed during the time. The standard realization seemed to be blue jeans, particularly overalls, and flannel shirts.

Carson pulled her shawl more tightly around her, glad for the heavy material of her widow's dress in the cold morning, and took her seat to tell her tale.

"History tells us that it was Anne Butcher's love for a Federal captain that was the only thing that saved Butcher's Roost from the fires of the Federals. The Yankee captain insisted, once the farm was captured, that it be used as a hospital to treat the wounded coming into the area. At the time, they had to keep their romance a secret but he came back at the end of the war and the widow married him. They lived as husband and wife another twenty years and raised four children together."

Carson had seen the picture of the pretty widow and her handsome captain and she embellished the story as she told it, enjoying the looks on the children's faces.

Those wondering looks were the reason she'd become a teacher in the first place. Sometimes it was hard to remember when parents were upset over seating arrangements and homework assignments. Or she was being swallowed by the ton of paperwork that had nothing to do with teaching her class.

She'd become a teacher for the look on a child's face when they first learned something new. That awe and wonder that this thing existed and now they understood it. And maybe it was corny, but she thought she could make a difference in someone's life.

Everything hadn't gone the way she'd planned originally when she'd graduated from college. She hadn't been able to teach a grammar school class but she'd found that teaching ninth-graders was equally as challenging. That elusive man she'd envisioned coming into her life had remained elusive long after he should have shown his face. But she hadn't given up hope.

And though she'd been teaching for nearly two years and she wasn't sure about making a difference sometimes, the look on the faces of her students remained the same. And that's what kept her from quitting work as a teacher and going to work at the mall outside of town.

When the story was told, the children went in search of their families and Carson shivered on her chair, waiting for the next group.

The sun was shining fitfully through dark clouds that had threatened rain since early that morning. The wind off the hillside made her look at the terrible job of candle-dipping in a new light. At least it was warm beside the fire.

"You look like a woman who could use warming up," a husky male voice said from behind her.

She didn't turn around but she did shiver again. "I look like a woman who'll consider candle-dipping next year!"

"I think I can help," Alex volunteered with a laugh.

He disappeared for a moment and when he reappeared on her side of the wagon, he was carrying a black iron pot filled with smoldering red coals that put out waves of shimmering heat into the frosty morning air.

"That's wonderful!" she enthused, scooting her

chair closer to the heat source. She pushed her toes close to the side of the pot.

"Warm feet," he murmured, looking up at her from his position near the ground. He settled the pot into a rut to make it safer against tipping. "The way to a woman's heart."

"Communication is the way to a woman's heart, Alex," she disabused him of his male notions.

"Communication?" he wondered, catching and holding her gaze. "I'm sorry, Carson. I didn't mean to drop in on you like this. I was going to call. My phone won't be turned on until Monday. Then Robbie came down sick and begged me to take his place today. I didn't know you were playing Anne Butcher."

"You don't have to explain," she responded lightly. "We were only friends for a year. And that was a long time ago."

She looked down at his hands where they rested on his knees as he crouched beside her. They were large and callused, reminding her that she had no real idea of what he'd been doing for the last five years. Yet, it was amazing to think how he'd grown from a scrawny teenager to the man before her.

"I want to explain," he began, glancing at the group that was building up waiting for a blacksmith demonstration. "But I don't have time right now. Let's meet for lunch or something, Carson. Okay?"

Carson pulled her shawl closer. "That's fine. When you get settled in." She still wasn't ready to forgive him.

"How are your other brothers?" he wondered, his eyes focusing on her face. "Are the rest of them still around?"

"They're fine," she answered with a polite smile.

"Bragg lives just over the mountain and Jackson still lives here. Riley and Woods are here for the weekend with the reenactment troop. Campbell and Lee both live in Virginia."

Alex laughed. "I'm surprised none of you changed your names. It can't be any easier for your brothers being named after the army forts where they were born than it was for you."

She shrugged. "We're adults now. Not many adults tease you about your name."

"Thank goodness you were the only girl," he remarked. "Those names don't lend themselves well to the feminine."

"And mine does?" Carson defended.

He stood up slowly, all six-foot-something of him. Lean and devastatingly masculine. "I like it," he said simply. "It suits you. Let me know when your coals start to get cold."

"Thanks," she answered. She moved her eyes quickly past his legs covered in black wool, his narrow waist, and his flat stomach. The loose white shirt clung to his chest and broad shoulders. "I'm fine."

She would have to be something less than a human female not to watch him walk away. He had been her friend. There had been nothing romantic between them. But he'd grown into a good-looking man. He was muscular but not so big that he lurched, she analyzed, watching his confident stride. He walked like a man who knew where he was going and what he was doing. A different man than the one who'd left after his grandmother had died.

She looked away and reminded herself that this was Alex. It was all right for Melanie or Lauren to flirt with him but not for her. She knew him too well. She might find him attractive but it was in the same way she might find an actor on television attractive. It wasn't personal. It was just Alex.

She concentrated on her new audience and by the time she heard the anvil fall again, she was retelling the story of Butcher's Roost.

There wasn't time to wonder what had brought Alex back after all those years. Or to nurse her old grudge against him. The day slowly overcame its gray start and the skies turned blue. The sun was warm and the leaves on the trees were still golden and red. People flocked to the festival from Seven Springs and the county surrounding it. It would probably be the last opportunity to get outside and enjoy the fine weather before the long winter set in.

A little after two, as the tour buses were circling in the wide drive and a new group of visitors were starting their way through the grounds, Melanie and Lauren joined her on the hill.

"Who is that?" Lauren asked, seeing the blacksmith stoking the fire in the forge.

"It's the blacksmith," Carson whispered.

They turned and watched as he lifted his arm that held the heavy mallet and brought it down on the red-hot steel that had been in the forge fire. The clang of metal on metal echoed through the crisp morning air.

"I know he's the blacksmith," her friend retorted, "but who is he in real life?"

Lauren sighed. "Alex Langston. Can you believe it? Old Martha Langston's grandson! Who would've believed he'd turn out so well!"

"I don't recall—" Melanie began with a frown.

"He's been gone for years," Carson told her.

"He was always in trouble." Melanie nodded, recalling him slowly. "I remember him now. Carson knew him best."

"Well, he's turned out pretty well," Lauren restated with a curious glance at Carson's face. "And don't you even think of looking at him!"

"Me?" Carson exclaimed, handling the heavy material of her skirt with some difficulty.

"I saw him first," Lauren told her.

"You saw him in seventh grade," Melanie answered sourly. "You didn't think much of him then."

"Whatever! That was then!"

"If Carson wants him—"

"I don't think I said that," Carson answered briefly.

"It's always the outsiders that get men like him in a small town," Lauren fretted.

"She's hardly an outsider!" Melanie argued eagerly. "She's been here since high school!"

"I can put a stop to this right now," Carson said. "You can have him, Lauren. He's not my type."

Lauren made a dismissive noise between her teeth. "Not your type!? Yeah, right!"

"You mean he's a little too hunky for you?" Melanie asked her friend.

"I mean, I know Alex Langston. He and I were never more than friends."

As one, they turned and looked at the handsome, well-built blacksmith who was busy shoeing one of the horses in the corral. Interested tourists watched him in amazement and snapped pictures.

"Friends?" Lauren whispered.

"I remember! The two of you were always together. It was your first year here," Melanie confirmed. "I thought you were dating."

"Never," Carson said in dark tones. "I was more like his kid sister."

"Well, I never knew him that well," Lauren continued and turned back to Carson. "But I'd like to now, Carson. So keep off!"

There was a short bout of giggling as a few of the other ladies from the visiting reenactment troop rearranged hats and gloves. They fluttered about like multicolored butterflies, watching the blacksmith as he went through the movements of his assumed trade.

"Ladies," he acknowledged them with a nod of his head.

"Sir." A short brunette curtsied slightly, holding her long skirt with gloved hands. She was wearing a deep green velvet gown that dipped low off of her shoulders.

He put down his mallet and put his hands on the hips of his black wool pants.

"Can I demonstrate something for you?"

That evoked a flurry of laughter and parasol-turning while Melanie whispered that his eyes were the color of hot caramel.

"You read too much," Carson scoffed quietly.

"Depends," Melanie replied. "I'm married. You know—look but don't touch?"

"Not me," Lauren said tartly, flashing them both a look of blue-eyed determination. "I want the demo."

Carson and Melanie watched Lauren saunter the fifty feet or so toward the blacksmith, her hoop skirt swinging provocatively as she passed the saucy brunette.

"How does she do that?" Melanie asked enviously.

"Sashay," Carson filled in for her. "Lauren sashays."

"How does she do it?" her friend pressed.

"Practice," Carson supplied. "She walks for hours in front of the mirror."

They laughed, the sound floating outward on the cold air.

The blacksmith looked up from his perusal of the woman walking toward him and locked gazes with a pair of laughter-filled hazel eyes.

Carson looked away quickly, pushing aside a small catch in her breath.

Alex picked up his hammer. There had to be something he could do to make Carson forgive him. Memories of her were one of the reasons he'd come back to Seven Springs.

"So." Lauren finally reached his side. "You're the blacksmith."

"That's right." He wiped his hand on a rag before he offered it to her. "Could I shoe a horse for you, ma'am?" He flirted back with the attractive redhead, not looking at Carson. "Or would you like a wagon wheel repaired? I can do a demonstration of early welding for you."

Lauren's smile widened. "I would dearly love to have you demonstrate for me, Mr. Langston."

"We need you in the house now, ladies!" Mrs. Engstrom hailed the group from the whitewashed front porch.

"I have to go," Lauren said, winking and pressing his hand a little harder. "Maybe we can talk later. At the dance?"

He nodded. "I'll be there."

He stoked the fire in the forge higher then turned to the group who were watching him.

Carson ignored him as she took her seat and began

to tell the story again. She imagined how happy Anne Butcher must have been to see that her captain was alive, that there had been no real battle. But she hadn't been able to show it.

Any sign that the two even knew each other could have meant death for them both. It had been a miracle that they'd been able to keep their relationship a secret for so long anyway. To all outward appearances, they'd had to meet as enemies after a battle. One, the victor, coming to claim the property. The other, the loser, to surrender what was rightfully hers. All the while loving each other and just wanting to fall into each other's arms and be thankful that neither had been hurt.

It was very romantic. Carson smiled, thinking how often her family teased her about her mile-wide romantic streak. The anvil struck hot metal beside her and she frowned, recalling how many times Alex had teased her about the same thing.

But that was another time and they were two different people. Still, she had to admit she was curious. What had brought Alex back to Seven Springs?

Carson was relieved by another storyteller a short time later. She walked around to the back of the house, looking for something to drink. Her throat was parched from the acrid smoke earlier that day and the constant storytelling after the reenactment.

She looked out toward the hillside and watched Alex as he explained his role to a large group of people while he drew the glowing horseshoe from the fire and hit it with the anvil.

"Can you believe that Alex is back?" Riley rounded the house and caught his sister off-guard. "Wonder what brought him back?"

She looked at him then dipped herself some lemonade. "I wouldn't know. I haven't really talked to him."

"He's in good shape. You can't help but admire—"

"I wasn't admiring anything," she defended a little too heatedly. "I was wondering if I was supposed to relieve Lauren or if I was supposed to find something else to do."

"Yeah." He smirked. "Right."

Carson counted to three and sipped at her lemonade. "You know I like men with brains, Riley," she scoffed. "A few well-placed muscles don't mean anything to me. And Alex Langston—"

"—happens to be someone you cared about once," Riley went on.

"We were just friends."

"Maybe he wants to be more than friends now," he suggested.

"Maybe you've read too much into his homecoming. His grandmother did leave him a house here."

"A house no one's lived in for almost six years?" He laughed at her. "I think you should look again. He might have come back for . . . someone."

"Someone?" she wondered, glancing back toward the hill. "Did he say something to you, Riley?"

"Not anything specific." Riley followed her gaze. "But he did say that he wanted to talk to you about something important."

She put down her empty cup and frowned. She and Alex had been very good friends for a short time. Was it possible that he could have felt something more? That could be awkward. She had never thought of him that way.

"You could go up and talk to him," her brother suggested.

"I could," she agreed, starting to walk away. "And you could mind your own business."

"You're writing him off without getting to know him any better? He's not the same man, Carsy."

Carson frowned. "You don't know your history, do you? Around here, the first dance at the Butcher's Ball is always danced by whoever plays Anne Butcher and whoever plays Captain Michael Payne."

Riley laughed. "Trapped, huh?"

"Unless it snows. See you later, Riley."

Chapter Two

Carson spent the rest of the afternoon avoiding the hillside. She helped with the ticket sales and setting up tours, much to Mrs. Engstrom's chagrin since it wasn't part of the plan, but Lauren was swamped.

By 5:00, she was tired, and her feet hurt. The long gown with its wide hoop had long since lost its charm. She was ready to go home and take a hot bath.

Her head hurt from wearing her hair up so tightly. When it fell down for the fifth time that day, she left it down. She looked at herself defiantly in the small mirror that was over the bathroom sink in the ticket office.

Her cheeks were windburned from being outside most of the day in the cool November air. The black dress did nothing for her naturally pallid complexion. Its wide, starched collar had chafed the skin pink around her neck. With a reckless hand, she opened the top button.

Okay. she considered her foggy image in the bad

mirror. Maybe the widow would look a little wayward that evening at the ball. Her throat was definitely showing. But she wasn't planning on staying very long anyway. She would dance her dance with Alex Langston. Then she would go back to her own time.

She took a small comb out of her pocket and ran it through her long, straight brown hair. For all the wishing she'd ever done for it to be different, there was nothing special about it or the face it framed. Her features were too small. Her lips were too wide. Her hair refused to curl, even in the dampest weather. It fell to the middle of her back without the slightest hint of a wave. A fringe of bangs crossed her forehead.

She sighed. At least she had good teeth. Melanie's husband, the dentist, had told her so many times. She grinned at the mirror, then stuck out her tongue.

Refusing to consider the uproar it might create, Carson put the small black hat back on her head without twisting the hair up beneath it. She pulled the veil down on her face and decided that she would have to do.

Like it or not, she was stuck with what she had. And the Butcher's Ball and Mrs. Engstrom were stuck with her playing Anne Butcher for that evening.

"Are you going to the ball like that?" Melanie asked in mock horror when she emerged from the ladies' room.

Carson glared at her defiantly.

"Fine! Fine! I was just asking."

They walked out of the ticket office together. Twilight was settling comfortably on the old mountain and the plantation that had lived in its shadow for two hundred years. Most of the tourists had gone with the coming of evening. The craft people and the food vendors were packing up for their trips back home.

There were lights on the gates and around the parking lot to direct the cars out of the driveway. The outbuildings were already dark with the closing down of the park for the day but the Butcher house was a blaze of light.

The ball was put on by the town for the reenactors to celebrate a job well done. The Seven Springs Historical Society was known across the country for their treatment of the actors who came to help for the day. There was always plenty of food and drink and the chance for some music and socializing after the day was done. They put on a lavish spread and a good time. Most of the actors would be gone the next day to the next historic site and the next historic battle. But they always came back to Butcher's Roost.

Jean Weller, one of the coordinators, met them at the door to the house, shaking her head in disapproval when she saw the "widow." "Mrs. Engstrom's going to have a fit," she pronounced while several laughing couples passed them on the way into the foyer.

Civil War fare was the costume of the day but everyone had loosened up since the audience had left.

"I told her," Melanie said with a shrug. "She wouldn't listen."

"Next year," Jean whispered, "Mrs. Engstrom will have you stuffing cornstalks into the beds upstairs."

"Where's Lauren?" Carson wondered, changing the subject since she refused to be bullied into putting up her hair or buttoning her collar. She looked around the rapidly filling ballroom.

"I haven't seen her for a while," Jean answered,

looking as well. "But I do see my husband. Excuse me, ladies."

Melanie edged closer as she and Carson watched Jean greet her husband with a quick kiss on the lips.

"You should get married," Melanie told her friend.

"Only old married women say that," Carson warned her. "I still don't see Lauren."

"More important," Melanie wondered, "have you seen Alex Langston?"

Carson had to admit that she hadn't seen either of them. She hated to admit that she was even looking for them. But as she appeared to be drinking a glass of punch and nonchalantly surveying the room, she was looking for Alex and Lauren.

It would be typical for Lauren to latch on to the most attractive eligible man in the group, she considered, disgruntled. Then she forced herself to reconsider. Alex was neither attractive nor eligible as far as she was concerned. Lauren was welcome to him.

They didn't appear to be in the ballroom, and the musicians were tuning their instruments for the first dance. Maybe Alex didn't know that the captain was supposed to dance the first dance with the widow.

"There's Jake." Melanie waved to her husband. "Want me to hang around here with you until the captain shows up?"

Carson waved aside her request. "Thanks, but I can wait here another few minutes by myself."

"Another few . . . Carson, you wouldn't leave without dancing the first dance?"

"If he doesn't show up soon, I'm going home. With or without the first dance," she told her flatly. "My feet hurt. This dress is like wearing a big black sack. And I can't breathe in this corset!"

"Hello, ladies," Alex greeted them, coming in from the verandah just behind them.

Melanie smiled and muttered something about her husband looking for her, and she was gone.

"Captain." Carson nodded, feeling her face turn red with embarrassment.

"You weren't thinking of standing me up for the first dance, were you?" he asked.

"Well . . ."

"I know." He held up his hand, his eyes intent on hers. "Your feet hurt, your dress is a sack, and your corset—"

"Never mind," she finished for him. "We're both here. We can get this over with."

He looked at her quickly, his eyes moving, assessing her. "Let's see."

"What?" she wondered aloud as he spanned her waist with his hands.

"Just as I thought," he continued. "I think I can help."

"Help?" she said as he came to stand directly behind her in the shadows of the huge red velvet drapes that arched across the verandah doors.

She felt his hands unbuttoning the back of her dress, and she froze.

"What are you doing?" she hissed.

"Taking care of one of the problems," he replied calmly. "Just stand still. No one will notice."

She felt him loosening the laces of the black silk corset even as she saw Mrs. Engstrom bearing down on them from across the room.

"What possessed you to wear one of these things anyway?" he wondered. "You didn't need it."

"Mrs. Engstrom," she answered both his question

and greeted the woman as she stood before her, glaring her disapproval.

"The ball was to have begun ten minutes ago," the woman addressed them both. "Are you ready?"

Nimble fingers finished fastening the last button on the bombazine dress. Alex smiled at the older woman.

"I hope you've saved me a dance, Mrs. Engstrom?"

Carson couldn't believe it! The woman actually blushed to the roots of her curly brown hair.

"I'd be happy to! I mean, of course, Mr. Langston," she stammered like a schoolgirl.

"Are you ready?" He looked down at Carson's flaming face as he took her arm to lead her to the dance floor.

Carson nodded. She was too stunned to speak.

"Better?" he asked as they walked through the group of people surrounding the musicians.

"I can breathe," she agreed warily. "But, Alex?"

"Hmm?"

"Don't ever unbutton my dress again in a room with two hundred people in it."

"You have my word," he agreed, turning her into his arms as they reached the shiny wood floor.

The band struck up the waltz that Mrs. Engstrom insisted her ancestors had danced to on their wedding night. Carson moved across the floor with her partner.

"What happened to Robbie Wilder?" she wondered as they danced. "Wasn't he supposed to be Captain Payne today?"

"He had the flu," Alex told her. "Disappointed?"

She looked up at him with a frown etched between her brows. "I liked you better when you were shy."

He turned her in the dance, her gown sweeping out behind her like a billowing cloud.

"I was never shy. Is that what you like about Robbie?"

"I didn't say I liked Robbie," she protested. "I was just wondering—"

"—if I'd talked him into believing that the sniffle he had was the flu so that he'd give me his part, and I'd get to dance with you tonight?"

She stared up into his laughing eyes, feeling the heat from his hand at her back through his white glove and her black dress.

"Did you do that?" she whispered in awe, not sure what to believe.

He swept her into a turn again, their legs touching as they moved.

"Would I go through all that," he replied, "just to dance with you tonight?"

Carson started to smile but flatly refused. She'd been mad for a long time. She wasn't going to give in to him so easily.

"No wonder you won the war. Those are some pretty devastating lines."

"You're pretty devastating yourself," he said quickly as the dance began to slow to its conclusion. "That makes us even."

"Now why do I doubt your sincerity?"

He shrugged. "I can't imagine, since I've spent the last month practicing what I was going to say to you when I saw you."

"Alex—"

"Alex!" Lauren managed to float between them and claim the opening between his arms. "I think you promised me this dance."

"Did I?" he drawled, his eyes not leaving Carson's as she backed away. "I don't think so. I think I promised Carson a trip to the punch bowl and a stroll on the verandah."

"That's okay!" Carson began to back away but he had already moved around Lauren and reclaimed his hold on her arm.

"Maybe the next one," Lauren offered while her eyes fired angrily at her friend.

"Maybe," he agreed absently as he urged the widow at his side toward the punch bowl at the far end of the room.

"That was rude," Carson breathed as they moved through the crowd of people.

"Maybe." He nodded. "But I've waited a long time to talk to you again."

She stopped and stared up at him as they reached the end of the punch line. "You are unbelievable!"

"Thanks!" He flashed her a quick smile. "I feel the same about you."

"No. I mean, really." She tried to find the words. None came to mind. "You're unbelievable."

"I'm getting embarrassed now," he replied with a quick look around them. "Maybe just 'great' will do."

"You're looking especially pretty tonight, Carson," Mrs. Chambers said with her sweet smile. "And who is this?"

Carson took her paper cup of punch from the older woman and smiled across the table at her. "This is Alex Langston, Mrs. Chambers. He's playing Captain Payne tonight."

"Oh, the blacksmith. Of course!" Mrs. Chambers handed him a cup of punch. "It's nice to meet you. I knew your grandmother. She was a good friend."

"Thanks." Alex took the punch and smiled at the woman. "I still miss her."

Mrs. Chambers agreed. "I miss her, too. She'd be proud of you tonight."

"I'd like to think so," he replied quickly, looking down at Carson.

"Well, the two of you run along," the older woman dismissed them. "We don't want to hold up the line. Nice seeing you."

Alex escorted Carson to a spot near the verandah, away from the dancing and the bright lights in the crystal chandelier.

Carson sat on the gilt-edged chair with great difficulty, trying to find something to do with the wide-hooped skirt and yards of stiff material.

She laughed when she saw her gallant escort having the same problems with his dress sword and the heavy material of his uniform.

Alex finally removed the sword and put it on the floor beside him. "I'm sure there was an art to this."

"A lost art," Carson agreed. "One that I don't think needs to be revived."

"I don't think history teachers are supposed to feel that way," he whispered as though someone might hear.

"You didn't have to ask Riley what I do for a living! I would've told you if you had asked me."

"You didn't seem to be in a mood to *communicate* anything," he retorted, sipping his punch.

"Is there a reason why I should be?" she asked, getting down to the anger and hurt he'd left behind.

"Carson, I'm sorry," he tried to explain. "I was lost without her. I couldn't stay here."

She stared at him. "Don't you think I've always understood that? I've always known why you left."

"Then what?" he demanded quietly with a glance at the people walking around them. "I left you a note."

"A *note!*" she exclaimed, drawing a few eyes toward them. "We spent a year together here with no one else to turn to and you left me a *note!*"

She saw his eyes darken and remembered the terrible doubts that had swept over him when he was a teenager. Then she saw the control and maturity that hadn't been there then. Alex had changed more than just his appearance.

"I'm sorry," he repeated. "I couldn't have seen you and left you, Carson. It's that simple."

She swallowed hard on the emotions that tightened her throat and made her feel like crying right there in front of everyone. She was surprised and pleased that he hadn't stormed out of the party. The old Alex would have done just that.

"I've nursed this for so long," she admitted with a shaky laugh. "I don't know if I can let it go that easily."

"You know me well enough to know that I'll keep chipping away at it until you finally give in," he teased. "You couldn't ever hold a grudge against me."

"Not for long." She sniffed, glancing up at him. "It is good to see you, Alex. You've changed."

"So have you, Carson! Who would've ever guessed that you would be so beautiful?"

She made a face at him. "Considering that I was so ugly back then?"

He laughed. "Considering that you were just a child."

"Not that you ever noticed," she accused him. "You were always too busy looking at the cheerleaders."

"While you were dreaming about the football players!"

They laughed and sipped at their cups of punch, remembering those painful days.

"You know, I think Mrs. Engstrom's punch got spiked anyway," Carson said, feeling the warmth of the liquid go down her throat.

He shrugged, finishing his punch. "What the woman doesn't know . . ."

"Why did you come back, Alex?" she wondered, looking at him. "It's been so long. Why now?"

He set his cup down on the table between them and faced her. "Everyone has to have a place to call home. Since I left, I've never had that place, Carson."

"But you couldn't have any good memories," she argued. "You hated growing up here after your parents died."

"You hated it, too," he pointed out to her. "Why did *you* come back?"

"My parents were here." She considered her own motivations. "It didn't seem like such a bad place when I got out of college."

"Not everything here was bad," he responded in kind. "You were here. My grandmother was here. The rest was kid stuff."

"So you hopped on your motorcycle and came back?" she ventured, a little misty-eyed.

He grinned. "Well, I hopped into my car and came back. I wrecked the Harley the first month after I left. I've never owned another one."

"It's probably just as well," she remarked. "I hope you drive a car better than you drove that Harley."

"What about you?" he demanded. "You took out

Mr. Bizzard's mailbox the first time you were on the road!"

"You distracted me," she accused with a wide smile. "You were always distracting me."

"I know." He sighed heavily but there was no remorse in his eyes. "I was the evil influence in your otherwise angelic life. Bad Alex. Good Carson."

"So, what are you doing now?" she wondered, happy to have her friend back, despite herself. "And what have you done for the past five years?"

"Mrs. Engstrom is bearing down on us with Lauren not far behind," he said, looking beyond her with his smile intact. "I suppose we couldn't run out the door?"

"I've worked hard to be accepted here, Alex," she rebuked him. "If it means you have to dance with every woman in this room, I don't care. So long as they still like me."

"You've become ruthless in your old age, Carson," he judged. "If it were up to me—"

"I know," she replied. "You haven't changed all that much, Alex."

"Okay," he relented for her sake. "How about lunch tomorrow?"

"I'm working tomorrow. They don't give teachers time off for lunch."

"I'll pick you up after school and we'll drive out to that place by the old bridge for coffee."

She looked at him with his black hair and golden eyes and smiled. "All right. But I have to be home before six. I have papers to grade."

He helped her to her feet, holding her hands in his white gloved ones. "I think I came back just in time."

"In time?" she wondered, hearing Lauren calling his name.

"To keep you from becoming completely stodgy, Carson."

He touched the frown lines on her forehead, his eyes intent on her face. Then he saluted her and turned to face the enemy.

Carson saw him dancing with Lauren. Her friend's pretty, animated face smiled up into his. Then he danced with several ladies from the Historical Society. He was obviously trying to do what she'd sentenced him to and dance with every woman in the room.

She was yawning, tired despite the cold air from the doorway. When her parents suggested that they were ready to leave, she was glad for the opportunity.

Lauren and Alex were dancing together again. Her bright green velvet dress shimmered in the light. His dark head was bent close to her very red one as they spoke. They moved well together.

Carson felt a tiny poke in her side and actually looked down to see if there was a pin jabbing her, but there was nothing there. She found Lauren and Alex in the crowd of dancers on the floor and felt it again.

She was just tired, she decided. It had been a long day.

"Alex and Lauren look good together, don't they?" her father asked as they were walking out the door.

"Great," she answered, then grimaced as she felt that sharp jab in her side.

"What's wrong?' " her mother wondered, seeing the wince.

"Nothing," Carson said. "Just a pin or something jabbing me in the side." *Whenever I see Alex dancing with Lauren.*

"It was a surprise seeing Alex Langston back here," her father remarked as they drove home.

"It was," she agreed. She was exhausted, but her mind was full of memories and unanswered questions.

"He didn't give you any warning?" her mother questioned.

"I haven't had a letter from him in four years," she replied.

"Funny, how he'd just show up one day. I heard he's having his grandmother's house redone," her mother said.

"Really?" her father asked. "That old place?"

The conversation floated around her. Carson stared out of the window into the darkness. Looking into Alex's face had been like seeing a strange and yet so familiar movie.

Carson's father had been forty-eight when he'd retired from the Army. He'd bought a piece of farmland with a house in Seven Springs and dragged his six sons and seventeen-year-old daughter to live there.

The family had lived all over the world, moving as the Army required her father to move. Carson was used to being the new kid in school for a few months or a year until they moved again.

But when they settled in the small Tennessee town, she found that the isolated community was slow to accept outsiders. They were unlike the military towns close to the forts where people were used to strangers. They lived a sheltered life between the river and the mountains. It took time and patience to win them over.

Carson was a little wild. Being raised with four older brothers and two younger, she ran with them, wrestling and shooting with the best of them. She wasn't used to getting dressed up in frills or wearing white gloves to church.

When she found that the girls in her high school

class ostracized her for being different, she turned to the intense eighteen-year-old Alex Langston for friendship.

Alex was an outsider, too. He'd been sent to Seven Springs to live with his grandmother in the seventh grade when his parents had died. He was angry and hostile. His dark good looks from his mother and his golden eyes from his father made the girls notice him. But he was a stranger and he was always in trouble. Their parents wouldn't allow him to date their daughters. The boys hated him anyway because their girlfriends stared at him when they should have been looking at them. He was alone until he met Carson Myszkowski.

They did everything together. In that last year of high school, they sat in the bleachers during football games and booed the home team. Carson sneaked out at night to watch Alex race his Harley, and they spent long nights talking on the phone.

Alex's grandmother was seriously ill. Her small pension wasn't enough to cover her bills and her medicine, so he was forced to get a job at a local gas station. More often than not, Carson was up half the night helping him pump gas and change flat tires. She helped him with his homework, and she cried on his broad, thin shoulder when a boy she liked didn't ask her out.

Alex was tall and lanky. His midnight-black hair was untamable. It matched the light in his golden eyes.

Carson's hair had just been starting to grow out from the short haircut that didn't distinguish her from her brothers. In a family that size, there wasn't time for anything that wasn't regulation.

He teased her as much as her brothers, but with

Alex, it was different. Carson could take criticism from him that she refused from anyone else. They confided in each other their deepest dreams and wildest aspirations. Nothing was too silly to tell Alex. Alex told Carson all the doubts and longings of an eighteen-year-old boy.

Then his grandmother had died, and she'd known, as he sobbed against her, that things would never be the same again. He thought everyone had left him, that he was alone in the world.

Her family had tried to get the wayward young man to come and live with them after her death. They had all but adopted him anyway. What was one more person in a house filled with nine people?

Alex had considered the offer, and Carson had happily helped her mother clean a room for him. The thought of how great it would be to have him there all the time kept her humming.

Then she'd found the note from him on her back porch. It explained that he was gone. That he couldn't stay in Seven Springs without his grandmother. That he didn't know when or if he'd be back.

"I'll always remember you," he'd promised at the end of the note. *"Don't forget me."*

Carson had sat in her room for three days, refusing to eat or to come out. She'd played the same song over and over until her father had pounded on the door and threatened to take it off its hinges.

Graduation had been two weeks away. Only with her parents' pushing and constant demands did she make it through the last days of school and the ceremonies. Alex had been her buffer against all the strangers staring at her. With him gone, how could she face them?

They'd called Alex's name out during graduation, and the silence afterward was reflected in her heart. She looked at all the uncaring faces and wanted to scream at them. They had driven Alex away. He had no home and he was out on the road alone. How could they do that to him?

Then suddenly, five years later, she'd looked up and seen his face, and it was as if the years had never existed. She'd been angry and hurt that he'd written only a handful of letters in all those years, but talking to him, hearing his voice, was like putting on a well-worn sweater. It fit in all the right places and felt like home. All the good times came flooding back to her.

In truth, she couldn't wait to hear why he'd come back. Was he really planning on remodeling his grand-mother's old house? What did he do for a living? What had he been doing all those years?

There was more, of course. Was he married? Maybe his wife hadn't come with him. Maybe she was coming later. He could be a father.

She looked down at the red cotton nightgown she was wearing and put her hand to her side. Even without the widow's dress on, she was still feeling that jab in her side. Maybe, she decided, she had bruised her ribs. Although it only seemed to affect her when she thought about Alex with another woman. But that was ridiculous.

She glanced at the phone, wishing that it was as easy as it had once been to pick it up and talk to him all night. It was a reminder to her that, although it was like he'd never left, he had been gone a long time. There was a lot of distance and time between them. Things would never be the same as they had once been. She didn't really know this new Alex and he didn't really know her. Their friendship had been between two different people.

Carson turned off the light and climbed into bed, sighing tiredly as she closed her eyes. She had never had another friend like Alex. Would they still be close as adults without the intensity of those teenage years to bind them together?

She was glad to be rid of all that angst but she had never been glad that Alex had left her. For five years, she'd thought about him being out on the road, wondering if he was still alive and what life had brought him.

For one moment as she was falling asleep, she recalled that spark of instant attraction she'd felt when she'd first seen him. When she'd looked up and felt his gaze on her, her pulses had leaped, and she'd nearly forgotten to breathe.

But that was before she'd realized that it was only Alex. Once she'd realized, she knew it was crazy. True, he was an attractive man, but that was different than being attracted to him, wasn't it? And she certainly wasn't jealous of Lauren! They were welcome to each other.

Chapter Three

Monday morning was cold and wet. There was snow in the forecast, but at that point, it was simply miserable.

Carson dragged herself reluctantly from her warm bed and forced herself into clothes and shoes and a coat. She gulped down juice and coffee before her eyes were really open, then she went out to start her car. She shivered in the cold car, waiting for it to warm up, looked at the gray morning, and wished she was still in her bed. Carson had never been a morning person.

Halfway to school, she realized that she'd forgotten her papers and books and had to go back. Before she got home, it started to rain. Heavy, slashing sheets of rain. By the time she ran through the rain a third time to get into the school, she was soaked.

There was a telephone message left for her in the teachers' lounge. It was from Alex, reminding her that he was picking her up after school. She looked at her bedraggled white blouse and jade-green skirt. Leave it to Alex to call her on a day like this. She didn't want to go into the ladies' room and look at her hair in the mirror. Maybe it would be better by that afternoon.

She folded the note carefully and put it into her pocket.

She taught three regular history classes that day and one honors class. The day dragged by with the students looking out of the long low windows for snow and Carson looking for Alex.

By noon, she was borrowing another teacher's blow dryer and trying to repair the damage the rain had done to her hair. Her clothes were dry. Her skirt wasn't too bad. Her blouse was a little wrinkled but she would have to wear her coat anyway. She kept a spare pair of shoes in her locker. She exchanged her soaked ones for the black ones with the low heels.

She was as bad as she had ever been, waiting for him to call or to come by. There had always been something that she couldn't wait to tell him or something that he couldn't wait to tell her. Between them, there was rarely a silent moment.

It was silly, she chided herself, to think that things would be the same. Still, she waited with breathless anticipation for the end of the day, and when it was over, she waited inside the school doors for a glimpse of him.

Worrying about what he would think of her was something new and she didn't examine it too closely. They'd hung out together in old blue jeans and flannel shirts when they were teenagers. She didn't recall ever worrying about her hair or her makeup.

She was an adult now, she told herself. It was different. It had nothing to do with Alex. She didn't even own an old flannel shirt anymore.

Still, when she saw him pull up, she felt her heart give a painful lurch in her chest. Then the stabbing pain in her side made her clutch her ribs. Getting to know Alex again was proving to be a painful experience.

When he unfolded himself from the beat-up, old black Corvette, she couldn't contain herself anymore and she ran out of the door to meet him.

"Hi," she began, catching herself as she was running down the stairs. She stood still and looked at him in the fading light, trying to see something of the teenage boy she'd known.

The black jacket he wore made his large shoulders look even more powerful, and his long legs were in black jeans. His hair was a little longer than a stockbroker might have worn it. It was thick at his neck where it brushed his collar. Definitely longer than any male teacher in Seven Springs wore his hair. He still wore his old air of arrogance and uncaring defiance but there was a maturity to his features and a control to his movements. She had glimpsed a part of that last night.

His golden eyes still roamed restlessly around him. Another teacher leaving for the day, Miss Starr, the kindergarten teacher, stopped as she passed him. He smiled and she moved in closer to give him detailed instructions on finding the school that was immediately in front of him.

"There she is now," Miss Starr said when she saw Carson standing on the stairs.

"Thanks," Alex said, smiling again.

"Any time," Miss Starr pledged with a sigh and a last glance.

Carson shook her head. *That* part of Alex's personality hadn't changed. But now the women of Seven Springs wouldn't be restricted by their parents from dating him.

If he isn't married and someone's father, she reminded herself.

He looked up. "Hi! Nice of it to stop raining for a minute or two."

"Have trouble finding the school?" she asked dubiously.

He looked back at Miss Starr's retreating figure. "Nice lady."

Carson didn't reply. Instead, she looked doubtfully at his car. "I could drive, Alex."

"Which late-model Honda is yours?" he asked sarcastically, looking at the teachers' parking lot.

She had to admit that there were a lot of late-model Hondas in the lot. But not to him. "Fine." She breezed by him to the passenger's side door. "I'm old. I've lived my life."

Alex laughed. "My insurance is paid up, if that makes you feel any better."

The inside of the car was cluttered with papers and maps and empty soda bottles. The upholstery had seen better days. Carson wasn't sure about the floorboards. Was that the road she could see through the mat?

The Corvette started, roaring to life when he turned the key. A cloud of smoke enfolded them. He grinned at her and they were off.

"The speed limit's only thirty-five through here," she told him dully.

"Relax," he advised. "I haven't killed anyone yet."

"What about maiming?"

He chuckled. "That's another story."

She laughed. "I don't know how to break this to you, but this is no better than the Harley."

"At least it's warm and dry," he rebuked her.

"I give up." She shook her head. "You're still a terror. Only an older one with . . . is that gray hair, Alex?"

He glanced at her intent face, her eyes sparkling as she teased him. He smiled his devastating smile. "It better not be. I paid a fortune for this color."

Carson swallowed hard and managed to laugh but the truth was that his smile had crept up her spine and sizzled the hair at the base of her neck. She subsided back into her seat, glad for the seat belt as they raced down the old back roads. She didn't want to think what it meant that he had that affect on her. Maybe she was catching some awful flu bug.

"This brings back so many memories," he said. "Being back here is like taking a step back in time."

"Seven Springs, home of *The Twilight Zone*?" she quipped.

"Yeah." He laughed. "Exactly. It's surprising how much you miss when you're gone."

"I never thought I'd hear you say that," she told him. "It was more like Seven Springs, home of misery."

They drove into the parking lot of the little restaurant that was perched above the river. The old building looked pretty much as it had when they used to meet there, a little more run down, if it was possible. The weathered wooden siding was gray now instead of brown, and the sign that used to be neon was just painted letters spelling NEMO'S now.

Carson opened her door and tried to get the seat belt off but it had a mind of its own.

"Getting out?" Alex asked, holding the car door.

"I was," she retorted, "but the seat belt seems to have other ideas."

"Let me see," he offered, crouching down beside her, his fingers working on the narrow belt.

She watched him, the look of intense concentration on his face, the shadows that combed through his hair as it fell across his forehead.

It was a strange, light-headed feeling having him so near. For all the times she'd cried on that shoulder, she wouldn't have believed that she could feel . . . something else that she was hesitant to give a name.

He rested one hand on her arm and looked up into her face. "Sorry, Carson. I guess no one's used this for so long, it's stuck."

Carson nodded, not trusting herself to speak. What was wrong with her? This was only Alex. Good old Alex who'd spent the night on her bedroom floor and given her his jacket to wear after they'd gone swimming at the hot springs. He knew her innermost thoughts, things she had never told another human being. She knew things about him that he probably didn't remember telling her.

"There!" He finally got the belt to open, brushing a strand of her hair from the shoulder strap as it released her.

Carson darted from the car as though it were on fire. When he looked at her curiously, she stammered, "I'm really hungry."

He had been gone so long, she considered as they walked more sedately into the restaurant. She didn't really know him that well anymore. It was different.

She wasn't a seventeen-year-old girl. He wasn't her teenage companion. It was confusing.

They sat at a table directly over the river where they could see the water below them. It was dusky and quiet in the nearly deserted restaurant. The waiter complimented them on their sense of timing.

"Everyone else stayed home tonight," he shared. "Afraid of the snow, I guess."

"It's not going to snow tonight," Alex promised him. "What's good?"

They ordered, and the waiter brought them their appetizers. The dishes sparkled with highlights in the candlelight on the table.

"So, how's teaching?" he wondered.

"All right," she replied lightly. "Sometimes better than others. What about you, Alex? What do you do?"

"I write computer software. I went into business with a friend from the Army last year," he explained. "That's when I started thinking about coming back here."

"You were in the Army?"

He nodded. "For three years. It was the best three years of my life. I learned more about myself during that three years than I had my whole life."

"So you can work anywhere," she admired. "That must be nice on cold, wet mornings."

He grinned. "It is, Carson. And it's the perfect thing for me. People actually pay me for my weird ideas."

"You must make a fortune," she enjoined.

He just laughed. "I've missed you," he said with a shake of his dark head. "I have so much to tell you. It seems like I've been storing it up forever."

She looked down at the marred wooden tabletop. Somewhere in that restaurant was a table with their initials on it. Not together, of course. Only couples did that sort of thing. They had put their initials on separate parts of the table.

"Why didn't you let me know what was happening, Alex? That first year, I thought about you so often, wondering if you were alive or dead. Then suddenly I'd get a letter. 'Hi. How are you doing? I'm in Omaha.' "

He fiddled with the salt shaker, not looking up at her. "I didn't want to come back a failure, Carson. I wanted to come back and be somebody."

"You always *were* somebody," she defended. "You just didn't think so."

"Isn't that all that matters?" he asked, catching her gaze. "I couldn't come back here until I knew that I was going to make it."

"A phone call wouldn't have stopped you," she replied tartly.

He smiled. "I wanted to see you. I wanted to talk to you. But not until I was ready to come back. I went through some pretty bad times on the road. I didn't want you to know about them."

She shrugged and sipped her wine. "That makes about as much sense as most of the things I remember you telling me."

"Carson," he began in a more serious tone. "I came back for an important reason. I need your help."

She leaned forward, her eyes intent on his. "I'm not going with you to steal any of Mr. Randolph's moonshine."

"I came back to settle down here. I want to get married. Have a family."

For an instant, she was stunned. She quickly schooled her face and smiled brightly. "That's wonderful! I was going to ask you if there was someone in your life, but . . . is she anyone I know?"

"No," he admitted, pausing while the waiter left their meal and refilled their wine glasses. "Well, maybe. She's not anyone. Yet. But I make a good living now and I want to meet someone special."

"So you want to get married and live here?" she asked, trying to take in the information. She sighed deeply in relief. He wasn't married or someone's daddy.

He nodded and picked up a bread stick. "I think, despite my memories of it, that this is a pretty decent little town. I can imagine living here and raising a family. How about you?"

"Sure, I want to have someone special in my life."

"I'm sorry, Carson." His eyes searched her face. "Is there someone I should know about in your life?"

"No," she said slowly, hating to admit it. He wanted to get married and live in Seven Springs! Her brother Riley was close about why Alex had come back.

"Have you been married?" he wondered. "Divorced?"

She picked up a bread stick. "No. I've been waiting for the right one. The right person. He was supposed to be here right after college, but he couldn't make it."

Alex frowned. "I'm sorry. Maybe I shouldn't ask you."

"What?"

"I wanted to get the house set up before I meet someone. I wanted you to help me with it."

She looked at him carefully, wondering just what it was that had changed between them that she could see and he couldn't. Or was it just her imagination?

"You're my best friend, Carson." He laughed and

took her hand in his. "You're my *only* friend, Carson, and I'm lucky that you're a woman because I'd feel silly asking some ex-football player for this."

"I'll be glad to help, Alex," she told him generously, privately wondering how she was supposed to advise him on another woman's house when she didn't even know her.

"I knew I could count on you," he replied, squeezing her hand gently. "I want to have everything set up perfectly."

"Do you have someone in mind?" Carson asked, knowing she'd be sorry.

"I was hoping you might be able to help with that, too," he answered. "You know, point out the great single ladies. What about Miss Starr? She seemed nice."

"Of course," Carson agreed with her teeth set. "She's very nice."

"Single?" he continued, oblivious to the noise her teeth made grinding together.

"*Very!* I mean, yes, she's single."

He nodded. "Do you like her?"

She viciously stabbed a noodle with her fork. "She's nice. She dates a lot. I think she'd like to get married."

He looked at her innocently. "There's nothing wrong with that."

She stared at him, ready to speak. Her gaze dropped to his mouth for just an instant and she forgot what she was going to say.

"Carson?"

"That's great," she muttered, realizing suddenly that she was staring at him. "Are you, uh, actively going to look for a wife? Take out a want ad or something?"

He laughed and sat back in his seat. "I can tell you think this is a *wonderful* idea!"

"I'm just jealous," she told him quickly. "You know what you want."

"It's true," he answered in a whisper. "Someone just like *you*."

"Me?"

He looked at her. "Someone I can talk to. Someone I can feel comfortable with. Someone who'll stand by me even when I'm wrong or I do something crazy."

"Oh."

"What about you?"

"Me?" She gulped.

"Who are you looking for?"

Someone like you, a small voice replied, but she didn't let those words come out of her mouth. The conversation was awkward enough.

"I don't know," she lied. "That's why I'm jealous."

Carson couldn't eat another bite. She had the waiter put the rest of her meal in a doggy bag.

"I have to get home and do some work," she told him quickly. "We can't all work when we want to."

"You have to come out to the house with me and tell me what you think so far," he corrected. "I don't want to do anything else until I get some input from you."

Carson looked at him sharply. It was early, she argued to herself, chewing her bottom lip. Maybe seeing the house, spending a little more time with him, would put her back on more even footing with their relationship.

He was her friend. She was happy for him. But she felt as though she'd just gone to the dentist and had a root canal.

"Okay, let's go," she agreed finally.

"Thanks, Carson." He stood up beside her and helped her with her coat. "This means a lot to me."

"Good." She grimaced as her hair was caught in the collar of her coat. "You can buy me a computer and design some software for me."

He put his hands on the side of her head and slid his fingers through her hair to free it from the back of the coat.

"I've wanted to do that since I saw you," he told her, their faces close together. "You have beautiful hair."

"Thanks," she choked out, trying to sound irritated and managing to sound as though she'd swallowed a frog.

"It's strange seeing you with it so long. I always pictured you with that terrible chop job your mother gave you."

"That was a long time ago," she corrected him.

They squabbled briefly over who was going to pay for the meal, finally coming to an agreement that she would buy him a meal in the future.

"I think you owe me one anyway," she agreed when she saw she couldn't win.

"You mean for helping me?" he asked as they walked outside into the cold night.

"No. I think I bought the last meal we shared before you left," she retorted sourly.

He whistled as he held open the car door for her. "You have a long memory."

She looked at him as he waited for her to get in the car. "You don't have to hold the door for me, Alex."

"If you want to get out again, I think you'd better let me fasten your seat belt this time."

She sat down and waited patiently, even when he leaned over her, his body warm against the onslaught of cold air.

She closed her eyes and breathed in the warm smell of his spicy aftershave, and some soap she couldn't name.

It was making her nervous, this strange, over-powering feeling she had for him. She'd missed him but this was something more. Something that made her think about touching him, putting her hand out and threading it through his hair as he had touched her.

"All set," he finished, moving away before her restless fingers could match her mind's goal.

"Great," she whispered as he closed the door and let himself in the other side. "Great."

She listened with half an ear as he talked about the house and his plans for the future. Maybe she was turning into what they used to call a spinster, she considered as they drove out toward his house.

A spinster was a woman who'd gone past her own prime without finding anyone to love and begrudged everyone else the opportunity. Maybe that was what was wrong with her.

Or maybe, she'd just gone too long without a date. It had been a month since she'd let Tom Mace, the vice principal, take her to dinner and a show. He'd kissed her good night on the back porch, and she'd decided she wouldn't let it happen again.

Maybe she needed to expand her dating opportunities, she thought. Maybe she'd go with Riley to the next reenactment and hope to find a nice Confederate soldier.

"I hope I'm not boring you," Alex drawled from the seat beside her.

"Sorry?"

"Where were you just then?" he wondered.

"I was just thinking that you deserve someone nice to love you," she replied. "You deserve someone, Alex."

"Thanks. So do you."

"Well, maybe it will work out for both of us," she said quietly into the darkness.

"I can't believe in almost six years, with college and everything, that you haven't been serious about anyone," he ventured, turning the car down the side road that led to his house.

"I know," she agreed seriously. "It seemed like everyone I met wasn't—"

"Wasn't?" he prompted when she stopped suddenly.

You, she'd started to say. *Like you*. Then she changed it to, "The right person."

She needed to go home. She needed to be alone and sort through what was wrong with her. Why was she thinking about Alex that way? In all the years he'd been gone, she'd never thought about him romantically. Why would she start the minute he came back?

"What kind of software do you write?" she asked, trying to get the conversation back on a level she could understand.

He stopped outside the darkened house and turned to face her in the warm interior of the car. "Whatever kind sells," he answered simply. "Is something wrong, Carson?"

"Yes," she paused. "No. I don't know, Alex. Its been so long, and suddenly you're back, and it's like you've never been gone."

"Is that bad?" he queried.

"I don't know," she responded truthfully. "It's confusing."

He took a deep breath. "I guess I'm taking all of this for granted. When I came back, I felt as though I hadn't ever left. I didn't mean to spring everything on you so quickly."

"It's okay," she reassured him. "I'll live. Let's go in and take a look at the house."

"Are you sure? We can wait. I don't want to rush you."

She sighed. "I'm as ready as I'm ever going to be, Alex. It's either now or never."

"All right," he said grimly. "Let's go."

The seat belt released as Alex had told her. He opened the car door and she followed him up the path toward the house.

"You could have left a light on," she grumbled, stumbling over something in the darkness. "How are we supposed to see?" Carson stepped over an invisible barrier and the house was flooded with light. She jumped back, stunned.

"I had it set up as a surprise," he explained, taking her hand and drawing her toward the front door. "Otherwise it would have been on already. It has dusk-to-dawn sensors."

The big old house had already been gutted and work on the new interior and exterior was well under way.

"Of course it does." She smiled, glancing at where their fingers were entwined. "Being a computer geek, I suppose it does everything on a program."

"Not everything," he demurred. "And I'm not a computer geek."

"Okay, nerd," she corrected with a laugh. "Oh, you can dish it out, Alex, but you can't take it!"

"And I suppose you can?" he argued, his breath frosty on the air between them.

She screamed when he picked her up and ran up the stairs to the front door. The door opened automatically, registering his presence.

"Oh, great," she criticized. "Someone comes up to burglarize the house and the front door opens for them. Only you could have thought of that!"

He acted like he was going to drop her, and she screamed again and held on to him for dear life. Then he walked into the house, and the interior lights came on around them.

"Oh, Alex," she gasped as he let her slide down from his grasp. "It's beautiful."

The rooms had been opened. The floors were stripped and revarnished in a lighter stain, giving the whole downstairs a newer, more modern feeling. He'd taken out the dark, heavy concrete fireplace that his grandmother had never used and replaced it with a huge stone hearth.

"I can't believe you did all this already," she said, walking through the empty rooms.

"I had Matt Carter and his crew over here before I came back," he explained with evident pleasure in his voice. "I'm glad you like it."

They walked together through the rest of the downstairs. Instead of eight small rooms, there were only four, but they were huge rooms, open and breezy.

"I love the big windows," she admired, "and the French doors in back." "I was thinking about putting in a terrace or a deck," he told her. "What do you think?"

Carson looked at him, suddenly afraid that she shouldn't be there before the woman he was going to marry. Would she like someone else to make these decisions for her home?

"Alex." She tackled him seriously on the subject. "I think you should wait. Maybe whoever you marry will have a preference. I know I would."

He shrugged. "I still have to live here, Carson. And if it takes *me* as long as it's taken *you* to find the right person, I could be an old man."

She walked into the huge great room/kitchen combination, letting his teasing words go by without a challenge. There were no cabinets in the kitchen, just a huge opening where everything would be set up.

"I left everything open so that you could help me decide on cabinets and appliances," he told her.

"Alex, I don't know how Miss Starr or any other woman is going to feel if you tell her that I helped you decorate your house!"

"I won't tell her," he declared as though it didn't matter. "You're making a big deal out of this, Carson! If you don't want to help me, just say so."

She waved his words away with an impatient hand. "It's not that I don't *want* to help. I just don't want you to be sorry."

It sounded ridiculous even to her ears and she knew that she was stalling. She didn't want to help him with the house. Not because of some woman in the future but because she felt even stranger standing there next to him in his house than she had in the restaurant. Her heart was pounding and her cheeks were flushed. She felt light-headed and dizzy.

She had to be coming down with something. In a day or two, she'd be fine.

"Carson," he began. "I wouldn't have asked if I

didn't feel lost in all of this. I know it's been a long time but I really need your help."

"Oh, Alex." She felt herself giving in to him the way she always did when they were kids. "I'm not very good at this kind of thing. I haven't even changed the curtains in my bedroom since you left. Maybe you should hire someone. I don't know how much help I could be."

"All the help I need," he told her confidently. "Together, we could make this a showplace! By myself, I'm liable to hang moose antlers or something."

"Okay," she gave in, hating the look of torment on his handsome face. "I'll help. But I never want to hear anything about whoever you marry not liking what we do, right? If that happens, you keep it to yourself."

Alex put his arms around her, hugging her to him. "Thanks. It'll be great," he assured her, his face very near her own.

"You have more confidence in this than I do," she said, her eyes a little misty as his cheek brushed her own.

He kissed her cheek gently. "I always did."

"And look where that got us," she quipped.

"Hey, we're alive and upcoming young professionals," he answered smoothly. "I think we've done all right."

"Only because we didn't get caught doing some of that stupid stuff we did because you thought it was a good idea."

They stood together, absorbing each other's warmth in the chilly house.

Carson wanted to let him go, but her arms wouldn't cooperate. She was pressed against him with the shelter of their coats between them. She rested her head on his shoulder.

"You haven't grown," she observed softly. "Taller, I mean. I remember standing this way a few times and you always fit perfectly. You still do."

"Perfectly for you to soak my shoulder," he reminded her in a deep voice, his arms not releasing her either. He closed his eyes and nuzzled the side of her head. "And you always smelled good. Like flowers."

She laughed gently, feeling a peculiar languid urge to stand there forever. "It's so good to have you back, Alex."

"It's so good to be back, Carson," he replied simply.

"Well." She sighed. "I suppose we should go upstairs and look around. I really do have papers to grade tonight."

Neither of them moved, and the silence drifted like smoke around them. "I suppose we should," he agreed.

Slowly, they moved apart. Carson pulled her coat together quickly to protect herself from the sudden chill after the warmth of his body. It just didn't help.

Chapter Four

T he stairs and the staircase had been refinished, with the last of the stairs curving slightly at the base instead of coming out right at the door.

"A friend of mine who's into feng shui said that it was bad for the stairs to end at the door like they did," he pointed out for her.

"I don't know about that." She shrugged, starting up. "But it looks good."

The upstairs bedrooms, five of them, had been reduced to three, with an enormous master bedroom. Two extra baths had been installed, and the attic had been made into an office area that was the only finished room in the house.

"I see you have all the input here," she observed, walking into his work area.

Huge windows had been installed that overlooked the valley behind the house. The view fronted the desks and computer equipment.

"I've already been working, so this was the first

room finished," he said. "I doubt if anyone will ever come up here much anyway."

"I like it," she began. "It looks like you. It all does. So far."

"Don't start again," he warned. "It will still look like me, even if you help."

"All right." She gave up. "But I need to go home."

"Sure." He nodded. "Thanks for coming, Carson. I have all the samples here for the wallpaper and the rugs and everything. Whenever you can come by will be great."

She glanced at her watch. "It's nearly midnight! Did you realize it was so late?"

"Pumpkin time?" he drawled.

She gave him a quelling look. "Some of us don't get to work from a cushy office in our attic! Some of us have bus detail tomorrow morning at six-thirty."

"I could teach you how to write software, and you could work for me," he volunteered, following her back down the stairs.

"I don't think so," she retorted. "Thanks anyway."

"So, how about tomorrow?"

"Tomorrow?" she wondered.

"To start looking over samples and making decisions on the cabinets and moldings. The sooner I get started, the sooner I can start dating."

"I know," she ground out, the front door opening as she approached. She had that sharp jabbing pain in her side again.

"So, tomorrow?" he persisted as they walked out to the car.

"I think I'm busy tomorrow," she lied. "Maybe Wednesday night."

"Busy?" he considered as he helped her into the car and strapped the seat belt for her.

"I do date, and have other social activities," she informed him dryly. "I do have a life."

"Really?" He looked up into her face as he started the car. "Who are you dating?"

"That's none of your—"

"Robbie Wilder, isn't it?" he questioned ruthlessly as they drove back to her house. "I knew you looked disappointed when I showed up as the captain."

She glared at him. "I'm not talking to you about my personal life. You always make fun of it."

"When was the last time you had a date?" he continued as though she hadn't spoken.

They sparred down the long road that led to her house, curving around the lake where they'd gone swimming at night in their youth.

Carson jumped out when they reached her house, not giving him a chance to come inside. She was tired. Too much had happened that she needed to think about without him badgering her.

"You know I won't give up," he warned her as she ran up to the door.

"Good night, Alex!" she threw back as she slipped into the house.

"Carson, is that you?" her mother asked, turning on a light in the foyer as she came down the stairs. "Your father brought your car home from the school tonight."

"Yes, Mom, thanks." Carson nodded. "I was out with Alex."

Her mother shook her head. "Have we just stepped back in time? I think I remember hearing that explanation before."

Carson smiled and kissed her mother's forehead. "I think we have and you have, Mom. Good night."

"So, he took you to his house and wants you to help him get it ready for some bimbo?" Melanie asked as they sat at a table in a small café in town.

Carson nodded. "Not some bimbo. His future wife."

"Imagine!" Melanie breathed. "I wouldn't want someone else to decorate my house without anything from me. I mean, if I could afford an interior decorator and stood behind him, nagging him all the time, that would be different."

"I know," Carson agreed, sipping her coffee. "I haven't been out there again since Monday night. He's left messages every day, but I haven't called him back. Now it's going to be the weekend. He's probably going to hunt me down and drag me back there."

"You could just say no, you know? Like, 'Sorry but I'm not interested.' "

"I could," she assented. "But he's persistent. If I have to face him again and he tells me that he's going to have to be alone until the house is livable, I'll probably spend every waking moment trying to get it right for him."

Melanie looked at her closely. "You two are very close."

Carson agreed. "We are, I guess."

"No, I mean, *very close*," Melanie added, wiggling her eyebrows. "Anything going on that I should know about?"

Carson took a sip of her coffee to avoid telling her friend about her strange new feelings toward Alex. "We're just friends, Melanie. Really."

Melanie nodded but didn't look convinced. She

didn't pursue the subject. "I was going to invite you for the game and the tailgate party tonight anyway. It's not much of a reprieve from decorating, but—"

"I'll take it." Carson grinned, glad of the opportunity to try to sort through her emotions one more night. "I won't even go home. I'll just help you get everything set up and borrow some of your warm clothes to wear to the game. That way, the earliest I'll have to face him will be tomorrow."

"Probably at the crack of dawn," Melanie related the bad news.

Carson nodded. "I feel terrible doing this to him."

"Even after he basically ignored you for five years?" Melanie debated.

"Yes. Even though he deserves it. I'm having a hard time with this whole idea. He's back. He's wants to get married. He wants me to introduce him to eligible women."

"Eligible women?" Melanie's eyes opened wide. "You didn't say he asked you about eligible women. That's my specialty! I'll be glad to set him up."

"I thought you had your hands full," Carson explained. "You've been looking for someone to set me up with for two years."

"But you didn't even like Assistant Principal Mace!" Melanie rolled her expressive eyes. "You might be hopeless! Alex, on the other hand, is handsome, working, and has a nice house. He should be a snap."

"I don't think I want to hear this," Carson told her flatly. "Anyway." She glanced around them at the windows of the coffee shop. "We better go. He might be cruising the streets looking for me."

"We'll take my car," Melanie whispered with a quick look around. "Maybe he'll think you left town."

Carson laughed. "You're crazier than I am."

"I know." Melanie preened, holding her blond head high. "Thanks."

They were in her house making snacks to take to the tailgate party when the phone rang.

They looked at each other. Melanie whispered, "Should I answer that?"

"It's your phone," Carson reminded her.

"But it might be *him*." Her friend opened her eyes wide and wrung her hands. "What should I say if he asks if you're here?"

"Never mind." Carson laughed and ate a piece of celery before she put the chunks into the plastic container. "Just answer the phone."

Melanie picked up the receiver and spoke quietly into it. Then she replaced it and came back to the counter where they were working.

"It was just my mother," she told Carson. "Jamie has the hives from eating too much chocolate, and it's not even suppertime."

"Maybe you should hire a sitter next time," Carson suggested.

"Just try to find one, especially on the weekend."

They worked together for the next hour getting food ready and packing coolers with ice and drinks. In the comfortable, familiar surroundings, Carson hinted at her strange feelings about Alex. Melanie stopped working and stared at her.

"Carson, no wonder you don't want to help get his house ready for his future wife. You're attracted to the man yourself."

"I'm not attracted to Alex Langston," she denied. "I feel about him like Riley or Woods. Like he's my brother."

Melanie shrugged. "Have it your way. But remember you heard it here first."

Carson went on making deviled eggs and laughed at the suggestion, giving it the scorn it deserved. No one understood their relationship. Even her parents had been concerned that she was infatuated with him when they were younger. Nothing could have been further from the truth.

She was still a little shaken from seeing him again and hearing that he'd come back to Seven Springs to settle down and get married. That didn't mean that she was jealous or that she wanted him for herself.

She knew too much about him. He was impatient. He was a loner and didn't like social situations very much.

No doubt that was why he'd decided to work for himself, she considered. That way, he didn't have to get along with anyone. Alex didn't care anything for anyone's opinion and he went his own way.

Carson knew she wasn't like that. Maybe sometimes she'd like to be distant and uncaring, but the truth was that she wanted people to like her.

She'd worked hard at it for the past five years. Working with people, being part of the Historical Society and a few other organizations were important to her. She liked people and wanted to be a part of things.

Carson wasn't even sure they were still friends. She had changed a lot. She felt sure Alex had changed as well. They had always been as different as two people could be and still get along. The only thing between them anymore might be the past. She hadn't seen enough of Alex to know.

But any other relationship between them was laughable. Carson and Alex. Yeah, right. They were *never* attracted to each other that way!

It was almost 6:00 P.M. when Jake walked into the house. Kickoff time was 7:30. Melanie was beginning to worry.

Carson had reassured her as she rummaged through her closet for warm clothes to wear. She finally settled on a pair of black sweatpants and a thick sweater to wear over her T-shirt.

"He's here!" Melanie jumped up, hearing the front door open.

"That must be love." Carson sighed, knowing the couple had been married for six years and were still very close.

Sometimes it rankled when she saw them together. Why hadn't she been able to find the right person? Melanie had found Jake. Jean had found her husband. Lauren. Well, Lauren's marriage didn't work out. She and Carson were always fighting for attention from some single man in the group.

Her parents had been married for twenty-six years, she considered, looking through Melanie's drawers for heavy socks. Even Mrs. Engstrom had been married forever.

"Melanie," she called walking out of the bedroom into the great room. "I can't find any socks."

"They're in the top drawer, left-hand side," Melanie said in an artificial voice that drew Carson's immediate attention. "Carson, look who Jake ran into and brought along for the tailgate party and the game."

Carson groaned silently before she looked toward

the door. Only one person could make Melanie sound like that.

"Hi," Alex said.

"Hi," she returned, tucking her hair behind her ear. "Excuse me."

She retreated to the bedroom with Melanie on her heels.

"What do we do now?" Melanie asked in a whisper, glancing at her as she closed the door.

Carson shrugged and slid a pair of heavy socks on her feet. "We party."

The three trucks were parked side-by-side in the Whitmore High School parking lot. All around them, the rest of the lot was crowded with other football fans laughing and talking about the upcoming game between Whitmore and Sun Valley. It was homecoming for Whitmore and a chance to settle the score with their bitter rivals.

Carson refused to take a folding chair when Jake offered her one. Movement offered her the best means of staying away from Alex that night. Sitting in one place, he was bound to corner her. How could she explain why she'd been avoiding him?

At that moment, she didn't have to worry about him. Alex was practically sitting with Mary Lou—she couldn't recall her married name—in his lap.

The air was so cold that the smoke drifted straight up into the sky in a single plume. She watched him through it, trying to be inconspicuous.

Why hadn't she ever thought that he was attractive? she wondered. Even when the girls in school were dying to catch his attention, she was happy to be his friend.

She decided, finally, that it wasn't that she found

him unattractive. He was a handsome man with his high cheekbones and beautiful eyes. His black hair was thick and unruly. The bane of his life, as she recalled from their youth.

And she had to admit that he was in wonderful shape. Lean but muscular, broad chest, and long legs. She traced him upward with her eyes and found herself looking straight into his smoldering gaze.

Mary Lou whispered something into his ear through cupped hands that made him laugh out loud. His dark face was animated, and though he laughed at what Mary Lou had said, his attention was on her.

"Nothing Mary Lou has ever said could be that funny," Melanie said, standing beside her friend.

Carson, glad for the distraction, looked away from him with some difficulty.

"She's doing what she always does and latching on to the most available man in the group," Melanie continued, unaware that Carson hadn't been focused on her words.

"He can't marry her," Carson protested in disgust. "She's already married!"

Melanie shrugged. "I guess she can't have *your* man. Oops! Did I say *your* man? I meant *that* man."

"Never mind," Carson responded, looking angrily at her friend. "I know what you meant. And you're wrong."

She knew Alex better than to think that he was interested in Mary Lou. He was with Mary Lou to annoy her. And it was working.

She watched them again. Mary Lou's subtle and not-so-subtle touches to his hands and face. Alex smiling and looking at the woman as though he intended to swallow her whole.

Carson remembered the ploy from another time when he was angry at her. He'd used that cheerleader, Cindy what's-her-name who moved to Utah to be a ski instructor. He'd asked Carson to meet him at Nemo's then arranged for Cindy to be there first.

He'd looked over her head at Carson the whole time he was whispering in the other girl's ear and watching her play with her pretty blond hair.

Carson had been angry but only because he thought he could manipulate her that way. They'd had an argument because Carson had eaten lunch with a new guy in school. She knew Cindy didn't mean anything to him. She hadn't been jealous, just exasperated.

It hadn't worked when they were teenagers, she determined, looking around to find Tom Mace, the assistant principal, looking at her. It wasn't going to work that night either.

She smiled in his direction, and Tom was at her side in a heartbeat.

"Carson," he hailed her. "I haven't seen you in a while. Where have you been hiding?"

"In the history classes," she answered, glancing across the fire to see if Alex had noticed her ignoring him.

"Yeah," Tom agreed with his horsey laugh. He was a tall, thin man whose best feature was his bright blue eyes. "They keep us pretty busy."

"Yeah," she responded. "Great night for the game, huh?"

"Yeah. You know, I never noticed you at the games before. I guess you just got the spirit, huh?"

"I've been here, Tom."

"Well." He laughed, stroking his hair with a careless

hand. "You look pretty good tonight. I've been hoping we were going to go out again."

"Thanks." She sighed heavily. "I've been, uh, busy." Even showing Alex that she didn't care if he was talking to Mary Lou wasn't worth this torture.

"I have a double blanket," Tom began. "We could share it at the game. It gets mighty cold up in the stadium." He moved closer to her and put a hand on her shoulder. "We could cuddle up close."

Carson was about to plead that she had a terrible headache or a contagious disease, when a husky voice interrupted their conversation.

"Carson? When you're ready to walk down to the field, let me know," Alex offered in an offhand voice that she knew was anything but distracted or disinterested.

He'd seen her problem and was going to rescue her. Just as she had rescued him a few times.

"Sorry, Tom," she apologized swiftly, putting her can of soda in the trash. "I promised Alex we'd sit together."

"That's right," Tom recalled suddenly. "You two were always together in school, weren't you? Are you still together?"

"Always." Alex stood beside her and wrapped a friendly arm around her shoulder. "Ready, pookie?"

Carson made a face, but she couldn't refuse his help or she risked having to miss the game because of Tom.

"Ready, sweetums." She smiled in return.

She'd made her choice to suffer with the devil she knew. She walked beside him down to the stadium.

The lights were on, shining brightly into the dark sky above the field. The Whitmore Wildcats were doing their workout on the fake green turf, their red uniforms standing out as they yelled plays at one another.

"Now Tom's going to think we're dating or something," she grumbled. As if she didn't get that enough from everyone already!

"Sorry, pookie," he teased. "If you hadn't been flirting with him to get my attention, that wouldn't have happened."

"I wasn't flirting to get your attention," she denied vehemently.

"Oh? You were flirting with him because he's your dream man?"

"I wasn't flirting at all," she continued in a calmer voice. "But if I was, at least I'm not talking about getting married."

"I wasn't flirting with Mary Lou," he retorted. "She was flirting with me."

"You were letting her because you're mad at me," she accused. "I've seen you do it so many times."

"Like you fake being sick? You're looking pretty well tonight for someone with a bad cold," he observed without looking at her.

Carson shrugged, wishing she hadn't told her mother to tell him she was sick when he called. "I felt better and Melanie asked me over for the party."

"Carson, are you trying to lie to me?" he asked, stopping and towering over her. "If so, it was pathetic. I've heard your best. That wasn't even close."

"I'm sorry," she broke down, shaking her head. "I don't know what else to say."

"Just tell me the truth." He started walking again. "We've known each other too long for anything else. I won't fall apart."

She watched him walk away, thinking frantically for

a way to explain that didn't sound like she was a witch. When she realized that she was going to have to tell him at least part of the truth, she ran after him. "It's the house thing, Alex. I just don't think I should do it."

"Is that all?" He stopped again, looking intently down into her face.

She was confused. What did he want from her? "Isn't that enough?"

He looked relieved. "I thought you were having a problem with our friendship after so many years apart. I felt like we were still close but I thought maybe you were having doubts."

"No." She put a hand on his arm. "I still love to be with you. But I'm afraid of you making a mistake with this house."

"Why didn't you say so?"

"I did," she reminded him. "You said it didn't matter."

They reached the stadium and found a place on the home team side. Alex unfolded the red-and-brown blanket around their laps, looking out at the field for a few minutes.

"Remember when we used to sit on our side and root for the other team?"

She nodded, recalling those long ago nights. "Or when we booed the team as they came on the field."

"Carson." He turned to face her, taking one of her gloved hands in his. His eyes were earnest. "I haven't been completely honest with you."

She swallowed hard and felt a tension grow in her chest. "What is it, Alex?"

"I had a relationship with a woman in New York

recently. It didn't work out. That's when I decided to come back."

Carson wasn't sure if she wanted to know any more. For the sake of their friendship, she gritted her teeth and asked him what happened.

"Paula wasn't interested in settling down," he confessed, looking down at their joined hands. "There was no relationship for her. I just didn't know it until it was too late."

"I'm sorry, Alex," she replied, seeing the pain in his eyes. "But I guess this is as good a place to run away to as any."

"It wasn't like that," he assured her. "It was more like waking up one morning and realizing that it was all wrong and that I needed to go home. I was standing on Forty-Second Street, looking up at the buildings, and for a minute, I saw the mountains. I missed this weird little town. And I missed you."

He chuckled softly and squeezed her hands, leaning forward slightly to kiss her cheek gently. "You were always there for me."

Carson groaned and closed her eyes tightly. The touch of his lips on her cheek still lingered. "I knew it."

"You knew what?" he asked.

"I knew if I gave you five minutes you'd find some way of making me help you do this thing. You could always talk me into anything. I guess I should be grateful it's not robbing a bank or something."

"Carson." He hugged her close. "You're the best."

Their faces were very close. She smiled, hoping she could make all the decisions on the house in one day. She didn't know what was wrong with her but she didn't like it. And it was getting worse the more time she spent with Alex.

He kissed the tip of her nose. "We'll get started tomorrow morning."

"Is there heat in the house yet?" she asked him grudgingly, knowing she was committed.

"They finished today."

"I'll be there by eight."

"I could come and pick you up," he volunteered, his eyes narrowing suspiciously on her face.

"I'll be there," she promised. "Just make sure there's plenty of coffee."

Everyone began to crowd into the stadium around them. Melanie rolled her eyes at Carson when she saw who she was sitting beside. It was an "I told you so" look that Melanie did better than anyone Carson knew. She was wrong, of course. Alex had come back to nurse his broken heart and look for someone who wanted to settle down. Carson understood that she was just his gofer.

Tom and Mary Lou found a place in a far corner. Carson shuddered when she heard them giggling under their blanket.

"Sorry you missed it?" Alex muttered beneath his breath to her in a quiet moment after the game had started.

"Are you?" she retorted sweetly.

It was halftime. The band was marching through the field. The cheerleaders were cheering while the homecoming queen and her court were waving from their convertibles.

"Have to give her credit," Alex stated, munching on some popcorn. "She's out there in almost subzero weather in a flimsy dress and no jacket."

"Now that takes talent," Carson agreed sarcastically. "If she could just sing or dance."

He laughed. "You're still jealous."

"And you're still ogling the cheerleaders."

"I never ogled the cheerleaders," he flatly denied. "I was too busy ogling you."

She stared at his averted profile while he watched the show on the field.

"You never—"

"Remember those red shorts you wore that summer? And that short black skirt?" He wolf-whistled long and low as he glanced at her from the corner of his eye.

Carson was nearly speechless. To think that he'd looked at her like that! Back *then!*

"I don't believe you!"

"I used your legs as a standard for every other pair of women's legs I ever saw after that."

Her face felt hot and something tightened in her stomach. Was he saying that he had been attracted to her as someone more than a friend?

"You never said anything," she said in a voice she hardly recognized.

"You were my friend." He shrugged. "I admired you." He looked at her closely. "Is something wrong?"

"No." She smiled, feeling the world right itself again. He wasn't saying that he thought of her as more than a friend. He was admiring her legs as a *friend*.

Did she need to make an appointment to see a doctor? She felt as though she had been through an emotional wringer. Her nerve endings were frayed. She didn't recall being with Alex as such an emotional roller coaster! Hadn't she been relaxed with him once?

The Whitmore Wildcats were trying to make up for lost time in the second half after losing the first half to the Sun Valley Sun Devils. Progress was slow. There was very little for the home team to cheer about even though the cheerleaders kept them shouting.

Carson shivered, wishing she'd worn more clothing. The air was freezing and the wind cut like a blade.

"Cold?" Alex asked.

"I think it's the concrete," she complained. "Why can't they build stadium seats out of something warm?"

"Why didn't you dress appropriately?" He sighed. "You need an extra pair of pants."

She looked daringly into his light eyes. "Got an extra pair?"

He grinned. "No, you could sit in my lap."

"Alex." She immediately backed down from her teasing manner and tried to laugh it off. The sound came out like a hiccup. "I don't think so."

She would have sat on his lap five years ago and not thought anything of it. She wouldn't have done it with any other male of her acquaintance, but she trusted Alex.

Of course, that was before she knew that he had noticed her legs! And before his smile made her heart flutter.

"I can't," she decided. "It wouldn't look right."

Alex laughed. "I did come back just in time to save you from being stodgy, Carson." He stood up, taking her with him, then brought her back down on his lap.

"There is one difference, though, Alex," she informed him in a choked voice as she tried to make light of the situation.

"What's that?" he asked quietly.

"I weigh a lot more now."

"You're right," he said in a strained voice as he

wrapped the blanket around them again. "I can't feel my legs."

"Serves you right," she told him, moving uncomfortably.

"Sit still," he urged with a laugh, wrapping his arms around her waist. "I'd like to watch the game."

The game had become a different one for Carson. It was suddenly very warm beneath the blanket and far from being more comfortable, she began to wish that she had never complained.

"I think I'll sit on the bench again." She started to move away but his arms held her in place.

"Shh! They're about to play."

His hands were warm around her waist, resting lightly against her legs. His thighs supported her weight.

The play went bad for Whitmore. There was a general groan among the fans. Even the cheerleaders looked dispirited.

"I've watched one game in six years," Alex grumbled. "They could've won this one."

Carson moved, uncomfortably. His chest rubbed against her back, the heat penetrating even through their layers of clothes.

"Keep still." He hugged her tightly suddenly, surprising her.

"I have to go!" She stood up.

"Where?" he asked, looking up at her in confusion.

"The ladies' room," she muttered, and walked quickly past Melanie and Jake to the stairs.

Melanie followed, almost walking into her as they entered the ladies' room.

"I saw." She grinned. "Tell me *that* was friendship."

Carson slammed a stall door closed. "Nothing happened back then, and nothing's going to happen now!"

"I don't know," Melanie offered, sitting on the countertop beside the sink. "But I saw the look on your face when you sat on his lap."

"Look," Carson fumed. "he's looking for the perfect person to share his life. And he told me that he just got out of a bad relationship. He thought they were serious. She didn't. He's my friend. He wants my help. That's all!"

"Not for you," Melanie murmured in a singsong voice. "I think you want something more."

Carson washed her hands and dried them with several paper towels. "I want him to be happy." She looked at her red-cheeked reflection in the mirror. "I want him . . ."

"You want him." Melanie nodded, her green ski cap bobbing on her head. "Now you're talking."

"I want him to have a good life."

"With you," Melanie finished.

"I'm going back out," Carson said. "I'm going to sit by my friend."

"Just don't sit on his lap again," Melanie urged with a laugh. "Unless you want him to be more than a friend."

Chapter Five

After the game, Melanie dropped Carson off at her car that was parked at the twenty-four hour café. Alex had driven his own car and had offered to take her home, but she'd told him that she and Melanie had something important to discuss.

"So, I'll see you in the morning?" he questioned, watching her intently as they parted.

"I'll be there," she promised. Alex left.

"It's not so hard to understand, really." Melanie ranged over the subject of Carson's relationship with Alex. "You've spent a lot of time together. You like each other. Then he comes back after all those years. You're both unattached. Bingo!"

"First of all," Carson debated desperately, "you've always told me that being friends with your husband was the best way to get a divorce."

Melanie shrugged. "I'm not saying you *should* be involved with him."

"Oh, Melanie." Carson groaned.

"Just that you *want* to be."

"And second, he doesn't feel that way about me."

"How do you know?" Melanie argued. "Just because he had a bad relationship? Maybe that's what it took for him to think about you as marriage material."

"He asked me to help him find a nice woman to date, Melanie!" she reminded her friend. "Men who are interested in you usually want to date *you!*"

Melanie shrugged, unconcerned. "He just lost one woman by being too serious. Maybe he's afraid of scaring you off."

Carson shook her head. "And maybe he isn't interested in me that way."

"And that's why you two are always together all the time, right? Because you aren't attracted to each other?"

Carson had ended the discussion by telling her friend that it didn't matter because she wasn't interested in Alex that way. But she thought about Melanie's words on the short drive home. It was crazy to think that she was attracted to Alex. It was harder to believe that Alex could be attracted to her.

Yet he had told her so casually that he'd been attracted to her when they'd been friends in high school. Or at least found her legs attractive. One minute he was reminding ther that they'd been just good friends, and nothing had happened, and the next he was telling her that she had great legs.

Of course, he'd explained it as the admiration anyone might have for a friend. That could be logical. She'd often admired Jean's coal-black hair and pale-blue eyes.

But she didn't feel like she was a cat on a hot stove when she was around Jean either. She couldn't account for it, but when she was near Alex now, she didn't feel *friendly* toward him at all. In fact, if she was honest, she felt something much warmer than friendship.

Was she attracted to Alex? she asked her reflection in the vanity mirror after she was home. Her face looked the same but there was a different light in her eyes. A sparkle that hadn't been there before Alex had come back.

Meeting him again was as wonderful as discovering a treasure that she was sure was lost. Talking to him, being with him, brought back all the memories. He was a friend, and yet he was more.

He was a different person than the boy who'd left Seven Springs. Not so wild. A little more rounded at the edges. He'd lived a long time without her. Done things he might never share with her.

Was Alex attracted to her?

She asked herself that question in the darkness of her room after she'd crawled under the quilt. She looked out of her window at the night sky, clear and cold, the stars far-flung across the heavens. Her room was still set up exactly as it had been the night he'd left. She'd moved her bed herself so that she could see him when he came to pick her up and they wouldn't run the risk of alerting her parents.

She hadn't kept it that way on purpose. She just hadn't thought about changing it. Maybe she'd thought that someday he would come back down that dark road and flash his lights three times as he had when they were going to meet. Maybe she was always hoping he'd come back for her.

She was tired but her mind refused to shut down. Feeling his hands on her hair, the least of his touches.

The quick kisses and the random hugs. Hadn't he always been that way with her? And hadn't she always accepted it?

But maybe, she thought tiredly, it was time to pay attention.

The alarm sounded on her clock just after 7:00 in the morning and she realized that she'd fallen asleep again thinking about Alex.

During the night, she'd dreamed about him. In the dream it was after midnight and the night was very still. He'd touched her head, smoothing back her hair. "I think you look beautiful."

She hadn't known what to say in the dream, but she thought about the look on his face while she dressed the next morning. The dream had left her strangely disturbed. It had happened the same way she recalled from a night five years before during the first summer they'd known each other.

The look in his eyes when he'd told her that she was beautiful was as baffling to her then as it had been so long ago. He had always managed to keep her confused, she considered as she put on an extra sweater. Why was it so surprising that it would happen again?

"Calling for snow today and tonight," her mother said as she entered the kitchen. The room was fragrant with the smell of baking cinnamon rolls.

"Sky already looks bad," her father offered, coming in from picking up the newspaper.

"Oatmeal?" her mother asked, standing at the stove.

"Earth to Carson." Her brother, Woods, whistled in her ear. "Come in, Carson."

"What?" She looked up, not knowing what they were saying.

"She's deep in thought." Her father chuckled.

"I was thinking about my car," she lied quickly, tucking a strand of hair behind her ear. "It was acting a little funny last night."

"Like the person who drives it," Woods added with a grin.

Carson frowned at him. "Can't you take anything seriously?"

"I sure can." He winked at his father. "When I see my sister sitting on someone's lap at the homecoming game, I take that seriously. Want me to take him out?"

"I'm going." She kissed her mother's cheek. "I'm having breakfast with Alex."

"Spending a lot of time with him?" her father wondered, not looking up from his paper.

That sounded too familiar. Carson shivered. "I'm going to help him pick out wallpaper for his house. He's getting married."

"Married?" her mother questioned. "Anyone we know?"

She shrugged. "No. She—she's not from around here." She stretched the truth like a rubber band. "He wants my opinion on some things he's doing."

"Is that what was happening last night?" Woods pondered. "Was he getting your opinion on his wallpaper while you were sitting on his lap?"

"I'm leaving," she repeated, ignoring him. "I'll be back later."

"What about breakfast?' her mother wondered. "At least have some juice."

"I'm eating breakfast with Alex, Mom."

"Watch out for the snow," her father warned.

"Watch out for Alex!" Woods laughed while his parents told him to be quiet and stop teasing his sister.

The morning was dark gray, the sun hidden in the

clouds. The mountains stood sentinel to the valley, black giants that seemed to hold the sky on their shoulders.

It was colder than it had been during the night, usually a good indicator of snow. She started her car then scraped ice from her windows, pretending she didn't see Woods at the window making faces at her.

It wasn't easy, being the only daughter in a family of six sons. She wasn't the eldest or she might have been able to gain some control over her rowdy, obnoxious brothers. They had picked on her from the time she could walk, making her cry when her mother made her wear a frilly pink dress and laughing when she went out on her first date.

She'd given them black eyes and learned to be tough from the beginning or she would have crawled into a hole and not come out. Her parents had believed in fighting fair and doing the right thing. Whether you were a girl or a boy.

She'd often speculated, when she'd been at college, that spending so much time with her brothers was what had led to her friendship with Alex. She'd never really had many girlfriends. It was easier to relate to boys. Yet not many boys saw her as a potential prom date, what with her gangly, skinny form, chopped-off hair, and ability to arm wrestle them to the floor.

And that was one hurt that had been worse than anything, she remembered, thinking back on it. Alex had left before the prom. He'd promised they were going as a couple just to snub all the girls who'd snubbed him and all the guys who'd ignored her.

She'd already bought her dress, a beautiful, full-length, emerald-green satin. Her mother had promised that she wouldn't tell her brothers. They wouldn't be able to make fun of it, or her, until the night of the prom. That way she wouldn't lose her nerve.

But the night of the prom had never come for her. Alex's grandmother had died, and then he was gone three days later. The green satin dress hung unused in the closet until her mother had given it away a few years later with her blessing. She never wanted to see it again, much less wear it.

Carson sighed, thinking back on all the little hurts of childhood and adolescence that could never be kissed and made better.

She pulled into Alex's driveway and shut off the car. She was grown up now. Going to college away from Seven Springs had made her realize how petty all those things had been in high school. She had friends and a profession. Someday, she would meet the right person. She would get married and have children of her own.

Alex was a part of that past. He'd come back into her life unexpectedly, but she knew that when he was married, their friendship would truly be over. He had been a unique, one-of-a-kind relationship in her life. She would always care about him, but she could view him with more equilibrium now that she'd had a chance to think about it.

She could help him with his house. She could even help him plan his wedding. Then she could kiss him good-bye. They'd had some good times but that was long ago.

"Good morning," he greeted her as she walked up to the front door and it opened for her. "Just in time."

She sniffed the air appreciatively. "Coffee?"

"And blueberry muffins."

She followed him up the stairs and into his office,

taking off her jacket and viewing him from a much cooler vantage. Hard-won maturity was her shield. Experience was her vassal.

"You baked?" she wondered.

"No." He shrugged, setting down the basket of muffins on his desk. "I microwaved."

She took a cup of coffee and sat on the sofa and he handed her a napkin and a muffin. "It looks like snow out there today."

He looked out of the huge windows and nodded. "I think it could be a big one, too."

So far, so good, she congratulated herself as she sipped her coffee and bit into a muffin. They were calm and polite. They were just old friends after all.

"So, where do we start?" she wondered after a few minutes.

"I have some swatches." He put down his muffin and picked up some samples, then moved to the sofa beside her. "I thought we could take it one room at a time."

"That sounds like a good idea," she agreed.

He sat close to her, his leg brushing hers. His head was bent over the samples on their joined laps.

She felt a momentary flicker of awareness, but she quelled it coldly, reminding herself that he was like a brother. *Cool and calm,* she repeated as they pored over the first bedroom. *No problem.*

"I was thinking about a big four-poster," he described. He reached for a picture and showed her. "This. Light oak, matching dresser and chest. What do you think?"

"I like it." She nodded. "What about the walls and the windows?"

"That's where I get lost." He shook his head. "I like

blue. I was thinking about just painting everything blue and putting up blue blinds on all the windows."

Carson laughed. "I don't think so, Alex. I always told you that you owned too many blue shirts. If I'm going to help, we're going to look at something else. What about white?"

"White?"

She nodded. "With some splashes of color. Maybe a throw rug and some pillows. Maybe even a border on the wall. It won't overpower the light furniture."

"Isn't white a little . . . white?"

"Let's go stand in the room and see the windows," she said, feeling, for once, in control of the situation.

He took her to the first bedroom. It was going to be a spare room. Unless he and his new bride decided to have children.

Carson looked out the windows, not feeling anything poking her in the side as she considered Alex with another woman. "On a sunny day, the light will be bright and strong. I think white with some color would be perfect. Something soft and breezy. Let me see those pictures and swatches."

She marked down her choices and indicated the room. This was going to be easy, she decided, feeling brave and empowered. She had faced her fears and she had won the battle.

The second spare room was a little smaller. The light would be coming from the front of the house instead of the back. She decided on brighter colors with white accents that enhanced the picture of the furniture he showed her.

"Naturally, we'll have to look at throw rugs," she told him as they left the room. "These floors are too beautiful to cover completely."

"Sounds good," he agreed with a small smile playing over his face.

"What?" she asked, seeing it.

"You might have missed your calling," he complimented. "You might be wasted as a teacher."

She laughed. "I think I can spend someone else's money as well as the next person."

"But you like to teach, don't you?"

"What makes you say so?" she wondered as they stood near the doorway.

"I listened to some of what you were telling those kids at the reenactment last week. Every time you told the story, you told it differently, as though you were reliving it each time."

She looked down at the book of swatches and samples in her hand. "I do enjoy it, most of the time. Sometimes it can be a pain just like anything else."

"I would've never pictured you back here, teaching history," he said honestly.

"How about you?" she questioned. "Do you like making computer software, or is it just a way to make money?"

"The first time I sat down at a computer, I was hooked. I could be whoever I wanted to be. It didn't have anything to do with who my parents were or whether I could conform to anyone else's rules."

"Then I guess that was love at first sight," she added. "You were always a rebel. Even your grandmother said so."

"What about you?" he continued, following her to the next room. "You weren't exactly a conformist, Carson."

"That's true," she agreed. "The only difference between us, Alex, is that I really wanted to fit in and you didn't."

"So you found a way to do it?" he guessed softly, his gaze falling gently on her face.

"Yes." She nodded. "I did. Next room?"

They walked across the hall to the master bedroom. She threw open the door, stopping at once when she realized that he was already sleeping there. The bed was the only piece of furniture in the room, but it was a huge structure all its own.

"Like it?" he asked, following her into the room. "I got it in Singapore."

"It's beautiful," she admitted, running her hand along the delicate, intricate patterns that had been painstakingly carved into the rosewood. "It's huge!"

He laughed and sat down on the blankets and sheet, still mussed as though he'd just climbed out of bed. "But that's what makes it so comfortable." He patted the bed next to him. "Try it."

"I don't think so." She pushed a piece of hair behind her ear and wished that she had worn her hair up that day. "I think maybe we should concentrate on the walls first."

"From this vantage point, I think they should be blue."

She smirked. "From every vantage point, you think they should be blue."

"No, it's the shadows." He patted the bed again. "Look for yourself."

"Alex, we're never going to get done this way," she said firmly, refusing to feel the faint flutter in her chest.

"Carson, you have to see this to appreciate it," he persuaded.

Carson knew she was going to be sorry. She lay down on the bed carefully, keeping her feet to the side of the comforter and sheets. They were blue, of course, she mused with a sigh.

"Comfortable?" he asked.

"Uh, sure."

"What do you see?" he continued.

She didn't see anything. Her heart was pounding and she wanted to get off of that bed.

"Uh, four walls?"

"Carson, look up! What do you see?" he repeated."

"A skylight!" she exclaimed, surprised that she hadn't seen it when she walked into the room. "It's beautiful."

"So the room could be blue?" he suggested.

"Maybe." She sat up. "Maybe a very pale blue."

"Any blue is good," he approved her decision.

"Alex." She turned and looked at him. "This is your house. If you want every room to be blue, it can be."

He turned and their faces were nearly touching. "If I'd wanted that, I wouldn't have asked you, Carson."

She looked at the small lines fanning out from the corners of his eyes, the slight grooves at the sides of his mouth that time had engraved.

"I don't think that scar was there before." She touched the side of his nose with a careful finger. "Army injury?"

"Hockey," he replied slowly. "It happened a few years back."

She smiled and felt herself relaxing, a deep warmth pervading her. "You've done everything you wanted to do, haven't you? Gone to Singapore. Played hockey. Found a way to make money that suited your unique talents."

"Not everything, Carson," he whispered in his husky voice, stroking a tendril of hair from her face.

"What did you miss?" she wondered, hypnotized by the golden light of his eyes.

"I missed having someone with me," he said without deliberation. "Everything I did, everywhere I went, I was alone. There were a lot of times I wished you could have been there with me."

"I missed you, too. I didn't do anything exciting like you did but there were a lot of times I thought about you," she replied quietly.

They were very quiet for a long moment, looking at each other, then he smiled and stood up. "Paula reminded me of you sometimes. In little ways."

Carson stood up slowly. "I can't imagine someone who wasn't me that would remind you of me."

He ran a hand through his black hair and stood beside her, looking at her.

"There's something about you. The things I always admired. You're honest but not preachy. Confident but a little shy."

"And Paula was like that?" she wondered.

He frowned and slipped a strand of her hair behind her ear. "Not exactly." He stared down into her upturned face. "I'm not exactly sure what it was about her. The two of you are really nothing alike."

"Maybe," she suggested, "it's something else."

He started to speak, looked a little exasperated, then tried again. "Maybe."

"So." She looked away from him with an effort. "Pale blue in here? Maybe with some darker blue and white accents?"

She marked it in her book, and he followed her out of the master bedroom.

"What is it with you and white?" he asked.

"Is that all the furniture you're going to have in your bedroom?" She turned back and looked at the huge, empty room.

"No." He shook his head. "I have some catalogues of furniture for you to look at. Maybe something that sets off the bed."

She nodded. "Let's take a look at the bathrooms."

"There's one through here," he replied, taking her back through the master bedroom.

They went over colors and fabrics through the entire upstairs, then called a break for lunch.

Alex insisted on buying her lunch at their place over the river.

"Is that snow?" she asked as they stepped outside. The sky was nearly as dark as the mountains and it was raining lightly, hitting the car's windshield and making a small spitting sound.

"Looks like it," he returned, helping her into his car.

"It's cold enough to stick," she observed as they pulled out of the driveway.

"It won't get really bad until tonight." He shrugged. "I can run you home if I need to."

She shook her head and laughed. "I think I'd trust my own driving first, thanks anyway."

"Are you saying I'm a bad driver?" he demanded, swerving a little on the small bridge that crossed the river.

"Oh no," she assured him sarcastically. "I'm saying that you're a terrible driver."

The restaurant was crowded when they arrived. The cold air rushed in every time the door was opened. They talked about the house for a few minutes while they ordered their meal, then watched the snow start to turn the riverbank white.

"What was she like, really, Alex?"

"Who?" he asked, then his eyes cleared. "Oh, Paula."

Carson stirred the drink in her glass. "You always sound either desperately in love or disappointed when you say her name."

"I think I'm just crazy," he acknowledged, looking down at the candle on the tablecloth.

"Well, we agree on something!" She grinned. "No, really, Alex. You said she was like me."

He sighed. "Not really. It's hard to describe, Carson. And it's nothing I ever thought about until I came back and saw you again."

"Could you elaborate?" she wondered, holding her breath. Was it possible that Melanie was right? Had Alex always felt something more than friendship for her?

"Okay." He looked up at her, holding her gaze. "She had beautiful eyes and long legs. Her hair was like silk and her lips were perfectly shaped."

Carson cleared her throat, a huge boulder growing in her throat while she listened to him. "Uh, what about her personality? I mean, what was she like?"

"She was smart and funny," he told her. "She was easy to be with. We had some good times together."

"That's a lot for one person," Carson added, in awe of the picture he painted of his feelings for her that he saw in Paula. "Beautiful, smart, and funny." Did he really feel that way about *her?*

"What about you, Carson?" he asked finally, after the waiter had left their meal. "What are you looking for that you can't find? I know you've had relationships in the last five years. What makes somebody the right one?"

"I don't know." She shrugged, picking up her napkin. "I suppose I like men who are funny and smart, too. Someone who doesn't mind debating things with me without always trying to get the upper hand. He wouldn't have to be handsome, but he would have to take care of himself."

"And someone who knows how to kiss?" he questioned.

Carson pushed her hair back off of her shoulders. "I'm not particular about whether he can win championships at kissing."

He laughed. "I remember that time you dated Johnny Twotoes. Remember? You said he kissed like a wet fish!"

"I was seventeen. I hadn't ever kissed a boy before," she confessed, glancing around the room and lowering her voice. "And his name was Johnny Tuoso."

Alex was in awe. "Really? You didn't tell me it was your first kiss."

She played with her water glass. "I didn't want you to laugh at me."

"So, how do you feel about kissing now?" He continued. "There's something about the way someone touches you. The way they look at you. Something that makes the back of your neck tingle."

"I guess that's what I'm looking for, too, Alex," she finally agreed with a small smile and a tingle that went from the back of her neck down her spine. "Someone who makes me feel special."

"Special," he concurred shortly. "And warm and silly and wishing you were with them all the time?"

Carson opened her mouth to answer, knowing her face was red but not from the cool air in the restaurant.

"Highway patrol just issued a special bulletin," a man said loudly as he entered with a blast of cold at his heels. "We're gonna get socked, folks. They say we better think about getting home and getting off the streets for the night!"

"Well?" Alex waited, a raised black eyebrow over an amber eye.

"Well," she said finally, picking up her fork. "I think we'd better get done eating and head for home."

"Chicken!"

"Eat your food." She ignored his remarks. "How's your pasta? Mine's great."

"Is there someone like that in your life right now, Carson?"

"You were always my nosiest friend!"

"So?"

"Eat your lunch," she said firmly. "And change the subject."

He looked at her again, studying her face as though he might be able to tell the answer by the light on her cheekbones or the shape of her mouth.

"Okay." He finally looked away. "So, when was the last time you sat on someone's lap?"

Chapter Six

Before they finished their meal, the snow had already blanketed the ground and was piling up on the road. They didn't get snow very often in Seven Springs before January, but when they did, it was something to remember.

Alex helped Carson into the car, making sure the seat belt was tight, and drove out of the slippery parking lot, down the hill toward the bridge over the river.

Carson kept one hand on the car door, feeling the tires slide along on icy patches under the rapidly growing pile of white crystals. She glanced at Alex who was staring ahead at the road, the windshield wipers working hard to keep the snow off of the glass.

"My house is closer," he reasoned out loud. "Maybe we should try to get back there."

"I can drive home from there."

He glanced across at her in the too-early afternoon darkness. "You might be better off waiting until it slows down."

"Then it might be too late," she disagreed. "The plows won't be out until tomorrow morning. If I'm going to get home, I'll have to go right away."

"Then I'll drive you," he argued.

"Alex, let's just get back to your place." She took a deep breath.

"I can't believe you're scared of my driving." He shook his head. "I've only had two tickets in my whole life, and I've never had an accident."

She smiled at him sweetly. "I guess wherever you've lived, they were pretty lenient about it, huh?"

Alex was stunned. "Carson, I—"

"Look out for that rabbit!" she shouted, pulling at the steering wheel when she realized that he was going to hit the creature.

The car skidded across the road and turned backward as it continued off the road and into a ditch. The rabbit hopped away.

It was as though it were in slow motion, she thought, when it finally stopped moving. Some bushes had cushioned their slide into the ditch, but the car had come to rest at an impossible angle.

"We aren't getting out of here," Alex said after he'd been out to look at the problem. "It's going to take a tow truck."

Carson groaned. "It's at least a mile back to your house from here."

"That wouldn't have been a problem." He stuck his head in the car door and glared at her. "If you wouldn't have grabbed the wheel. What were you thinking?"

"I was trying to save that rabbit's life," she reasoned. "If you had been watching where you were going—"

"I wouldn't have gone in the ditch if you hadn't touched the wheel!"

Carson climbed out of the car, a difficult maneuver since it was angled on the side of the ditch. She pulled herself up the embankment, wishing she'd worn boots instead of tennis shoes.

"Hey! Wait a minute!" she called to him. He was already walking across the field toward the side road that led to his house. Huffing breathlessly, she caught up with him. She had to start taking the idea of exercise more seriously.

"Wh-where are you going?" she demanded, tugging at his sleeve.

"Home," he replied shortly.

"You could wait for me."

He glanced back at her as though she were a fly speck. "You're here. No problem."

"Alex," she huffed on the cold air, "I can't walk that fast!"

"You'll get there," he said callously, without slowing down.

Carson wadded up a big handful of the heavy white snow and took careful aim. The snowball hit him with a loud whack right in the middle of his back.

He still didn't stop. The next one skimmed the top of his head.

That stopped him. Without warning, he started running back toward her.

Carson gave a startled yelp and ran back the way she'd come but he was faster. In one smooth move, he tackled her, and they rolled across the snow-covered field.

"I can't believe you don't know better than that,"

he muttered. "You with six brothers who could roll you into a snow woman!"

"I never learned to compromise or back down." She grinned up at him, her face full of snow. "That was the only way to survive."

"That much we have in common, Carson." He admired her, then sighed as he deliberately made a huge, perfectly round snowball.

"Let me up!" she demanded, struggling beneath him. "You weigh a ton, Alex!"

"I've gained weight since I left, too, sweetie."

He continued making the snowball bigger and wouldn't let her move no matter how she squirmed. She watched in horror as he concentrated on making the perfect weapon.

"You wouldn't!"

"Wouldn't?" He smiled maliciously at her. "You put my car in the ditch."

"I didn't," she pleaded. "Alex!"

"You threw two snowballs at me when I wasn't looking," he accused.

"You were walking away! You could've waited."

"You said I was a terrible driver."

"Well." She shrugged.

He hefted the snowball aloft.

"You aren't!" She took it back. "You aren't a terrible driver."

"And?" he urged.

"And." She looked at him. "And you look good in blue?"

"Carson!"

She pushed him away and got up off the ground, running for all she was worth across the uneven field with the slippery snow making every step slide out from under her. She didn't hear him behind her even though she knew he had to be there.

"Wait!" he called.

She made a fatal mistake and looked back at him. The snowball hit her in the shoulder and splattered up into her face just as her foot caught in a tree root. She stumbled back across a log, half buried in snow and grass.

The fall knocked the breath out of her. She lay still on the cold ground, feeling the snowball melt into her coat.

"Carson!" He reached her and skidded to her side, kneeling on the ground beside her. "Are you all right?"

She kept her eyes closed tightly, feeling her lungs begin to function normally again.

Alex was cursing himself and trying to decide if he should move her. His hands moved quickly over her legs and arms to check for damage.

Carson let out a loud whoop that her brother Lee had taught her to escape from her enemies, mostly Jackson, Woods, and Riley. She pushed as hard as she could, throwing a handful of snow at his head at the same time.

Surprised, Alex fell to the ground. He had to admit, she was good!

They chased each other the rest of the mile back to his house, letting themselves in the front door as the phone was ringing.

"It's for you," he said quickly, handing her the receiver.

She took it as he took her snow-filled coat and gloves. It was her father.

"The roads are really piling up," he said. "Maybe

you'd better wait out the rest of it there since you have a warm, dry place to be, Carson."

She nodded, watching Alex as he put on a pot of coffee. He was soaking wet and dripping all over the new floor. She looked down. For that matter, so was she.

"I guess that's what I'll do, Dad," she agreed. "My car isn't really made for this weather."

"If Jackson comes by with his Jeep, I'll let you know. Maybe he can get you out of there."

"It's okay, Dad," she assured him. "It'll give me time to finish the house with Alex. Don't worry."

"Everything okay between you?" her father asked in a hushed tone as though Alex might hear him.

"It's fine. Really. I'll see you later. Tell Mom not to worry, either."

Her father told her that they loved her, and he hung up. Carson put down the phone and looked up at Alex.

"Okay, coffee's on. You look frozen. I think I have something dry you can wear," he offered.

"Thanks," she accepted. "I'm really sorry about the car, Alex."

"Now you say it!" He laughed.

"Never give the enemy what he wants, when he wants it," she recited. "Lee's law of survival number two."

"You were lucky Lee was so much older than you or you wouldn't have survived," he remarked as they walked up the stairs.

"He did save me a few times," she recalled. "He was my guardian angel while he was home."

"Where is he now, Carson?" Alex asked.

"He's a park ranger in Virginia. He's married and has three kids."

Alex had only met Lee a few times. Carson's older brother was ten years older than either of them.

"Three?" He shook his head. "He didn't waste any time."

"It's been six years," she reminded him. "He could have had more!"

They wandered back into the master bedroom. Alex tossed her a big, fluffy blue towel then searched until he found a pair of jeans and a blue sweater that he thought she could wear.

"These must be pre-workout clothes," she mused, looking at the size of the clothes. The sweater would never have fit across his shoulders anymore.

He glanced at her. "The way you run, you need some exercise, too."

"Oh, no." She swept up the clothes and the towel and marched into the bathroom. "You aren't getting me near a barbell or an abdominal exerciser!"

"Don't you want to be fit?" he called through the door after she'd closed it.

"No," she answered quickly. "I like being a lazy, flabby mutant."

They sat at the table that overlooked where the terrace would be and drank hot coffee, watching the snow falling harder in the yard.

"My grandmother loved the snow," he mused, glancing across at his companion. "She was like a little kid when she saw the first flurry come down. I'll never forget it."

Carson empathized. "She was amazing. I remember her always listening. Even when we were telling her something preposterous."

"I remember my dad being a lot like her," he said evenly. "He always seemed like he had time for me."

Carson sipped her coffee. "They would have been glad that you're finally settling down and getting married."

"I know. Especially Grandma. She always said she wanted to be a great-grandmother before she died."

"I know it sounds trite," she said, touching his hand where it lay near his coffee cup on the table. "But I feel like she's here. You're bringing her house back to life. Remember how she loved this place?"

"Especially the garden." He nodded. "She used to be out there all summer from morning until night."

"Maybe we can do something with the garden. I noticed the rosebushes are still there. They're a little overgrown, but they could be saved. I remember how sweet they used to smell in the summer."

He smiled at her. "And I remember that time when you read in a modern witch's chronicle about gathering the last rose petals and using them to discover your future husband's name."

Carson laughed. "I was pathetic."

He turned his hand and gripped hers where it laid against his. "You were just . . . curious."

"It never worked anyway," she told him. "All that happened was that Jackson and Woods caught me walking in the moonlight in my pajamas and they locked me out of the house."

"You never told me that," he accused. "What did you do?"

"I climbed up the side of the porch and walked across the roof until I could get to the attic window." She shrugged as though it were nothing. "Then I put Krazy Glue in both of their shoes the next morning."

"I'm never having children." He laughed. "I can

only imagine finding my daughter climbing across the roof at night."

"Fortunately, I didn't get caught."

"Why didn't you tell me?" he wondered.

"Because I didn't want you to know I'd done something so stupid." She smiled slightly. "You were sort of my hero, you know."

"Yeah, right," he teased. "That's why you locked me in the girls' locker room."

"No," she disagreed. "I locked you in there because you were so stupid about Cindy the cheerleader. She didn't care anything about you. She was just leading you on, and there you were asking me to stand watch while the two of you were kissing in the locker room."

He looked down at his coffee and shook his head. "We didn't."

She stared at him. "You told me you did!"

"I lied."

"Why?" she demanded.

"Because." He picked up her hand and touched the tip of her fingers to his lips. "I didn't want you to know that she told me that I was a creep. You were sort of my hero."

Carson felt her face get hot, and the feeling transferred down her neck. She stared at him long and hard as he held her hand. Then, finally, she looked away.

"Well, it looks like we're snowed in until tomorrow," she changed the subject. "We might as well try to finish the rest of the house."

He nodded and she reclaimed her hand from his grasp. While he went upstairs to fetch the swatches and samples, she walked around the kitchen, thinking about him living there with some strange woman.

It was difficult to imagine. Alex and Lauren. Or

Miss Starr. Maybe children. Living in his grand-mother's house, watching the snow fall from the big windows.

She stopped there, putting those thoughts on hold. When he entered the kitchen, she stared at him as though she had never seen him.

"What?" he wondered, setting everything down on a crude table that was made of a piece of plywood and two sawhorses.

"Do you have a picture of Paula?" she asked quietly.

"Is that why you're looking at me like someone who's been taken over by the evil dead?" he wondered.

"Sorry," she apologized. "Do you have a picture?"

"Not on me," he said slowly.

"Not even in your wallet?"

"Not anymore," he explained quickly. "We're over, Carson. I'm not carrying some torch around for her or anything. She's not a part of my life anymore."

"But she was," she reminded him. "And if I see a picture of her I might get a better idea of the kind of woman you want to date."

"Is that what this is all about?"

She shrugged and tucked her feet under her in the chair. "You did say you wanted me to help you get dates with nice, marriageable women."

He studied her briefly. "I'm not looking for another woman like Paula, Carson. So maybe it's better that I don't have a picture."

The knowledge that she was helping him set up his grandmother's house for a woman he'd never met was not much incentive to do her best. Her heart wasn't in it, but she reminded herself that the sooner it was done, the sooner she would be free of the responsibility. Her obligation as Alex's friend would be finished when he was married and tucked away in his house with his new bride. Probably as well as their friendship. At least the way it was between them.

She couldn't imagine his wife wanting to see the two of them together when he was constantly hugging her or moving close to her.

She stopped in mid-thought. Wasn't that exactly what Melanie had said about their relationship? She had dismissed it as something that was ridiculous, but the tiny doubt had been planted, and she was having a hard time shaking it. It gnawed at her like the spring floods at the mountains so that when Alex reached across her to pick up the tape measure, she jumped.

"Sorry." He looked at her strangely. "Why are you so jumpy, Carson?"

"I was just thinking." She sighed.

"About?"

"The reunion at the end of the month," she lied, not wanting to tell him the truth. He would only laugh, she decided. She didn't want to discuss it with him. "I can't wait until everyone sees that you've come back."

"I don't want to go to a reunion." He shrugged it away as though she'd asked him if he wanted to be buried alive.

"It would be fun," she told him. "You have a good job, a nice house. There will be plenty of marriageable women there. Every cheerleader will wish she would have been nice to you."

He laughed as he measured a strip of wall that would be above the kitchen sink. "I don't want any cheerleaders to wish they had been nice to me. I don't even want to see them."

She frowned, holding one end of the tape measure. "You have to go."

He looked up at her. "I'd rather someone tear out my lungs!"

"I can't believe it," she continued. "This is your chance to show everyone. I thought that was why you'd stayed away so long."

"Not to show everyone," he corrected. "Just you."

"Me?" she scoffed. "I always knew you'd do whatever you decided to do. You didn't have anything to prove to me."

"Carson." He looked at her, started to speak, then the tape measure zipped back to its holder and he shook his head. "I don't want to go to the reunion."

"Okay." She sat on a sawhorse near the spot where his grandmother's coal stove had been. "I can see you want me to change the subject."

"That would be nice."

"So, let's talk about Paula," she commenced, swinging her legs a little above the floor. "How did you meet her?"

Alex looked at her, exasperation written in his face, but she smiled, ignoring it, and kept on talking. When she was talking, she didn't have to think about those images of him walking in the garden in the moonlight with some other woman.

They finished laying out the colors and the materials for the kitchen, and Alex declared that he was exhausted and starving.

Carson looked at the blackness outside and then at her watch. It was nearly 8:00 P.M.!

"So, is there anything to eat?" she wondered. "Or are you just torturing me?"

Alex put down the cabinet samples he'd been holding and walked toward her. "As a matter of fact," he began, putting his hands on her waist and helping her from the sawhorse, "I'll take you down to my larder. You can pick out anything that you can microwave."

Carson walked quietly behind him as he drew her toward the basement stairs. His hand was warm around hers.

The basement was just as she remembered it being when his grandmother had been alive. It was dark and cold and damp, and the floor was little better than hard-packed ground.

"Here we are," he announced as they reached an old refrigerator. He swept the door open with a flourish. "Your choice of fine microwave cuisine."

Carson looked at the ton of various microwave dinners that were loaded into the freezer and took one out . . . just as the power went out.

"Oh, great!" she breathed, standing in complete darkness holding a frozen dinner that didn't seem so palatable anymore.

"No problem," he pronounced, taking her hand again. "We'll just go back upstairs and scavenge."

"How will we find the stairs?" she wondered, not being able to see his hand on hers in the total blackness.

"Are you kidding?" He laughed. "I spent more time down here than the mold. At one time, I wanted to have my bedroom down here. Thirteen steps to the stairs. Follow me."

She walked carefully behind him, reaching out a

hand to touch him when she wasn't sure if they should be there. Finally they reached the stairs.

"Ten stairs to the top," he told her. "Ready?"

"I'm right behind you," she said and scooted up close to him. "Walk slowly."

They went up the stairs together, barely an inch between them. The light from the bright snow outside the big windows made the upper floor seem as though the power were still on.

"We made it." She stepped away from him. "Now all we have to do is worry about starvation setting in before we're rescued."

"I have some stuff," he promised. "If you'd care to follow me upstairs, I think I can keep you from starving."

They went up the stairs in the eerie half light, shadows from the falling snow making designs on the walls. Carson sat on the sofa while he rummaged through his office.

In that light, he could have been anyone, she decided, watching him. It seemed sometimes as though they had been friends forever. Yet sometimes, she felt as though she didn't know him at all.

"Here we are." He put his scavenged goodies on the table before her. "Two glasses, a half bottle of chardonnay, part of a Milky Way bar, and three peanut butter crackers."

"I'll take the wine." She grimaced. "That way I won't care if I'm starving to death."

In the end, they shared all of it, sitting on the sofa together, one at each end. The snow falling in the valley was beautiful from the huge windows in the back of the house.

"You know, the thing I don't understand," Carson

began after a glass of wine, her voice sounding very loud in the silence. "You have this great house. You have a job you love. You could certainly have companionship. I'm surprised you want to settle down."

"You mean like Lauren?" he asked pointedly.

She shrugged. "I mean, none of the cheerleaders would be turning you down now, my friend."

He smiled. "Thanks."

She felt her face get hot, and it had nothing to do with the wine. "You know what I mean, Alex. You always wanted to be free of conventional things like marriage."

"I suppose," he replied earnestly. "I don't think I'd feel right living in this house without getting married. You know how Grandma felt about those things. And I want someone to come home to, someone to share my life."

"A dog would do those things," she retorted.

"Haven't you ever wanted to have a permanent relationship with anyone, Carson?" he wondered, shifting his place on the sofa to see her face.

"I suppose," she answered thoughtfully, trying not to be aware of his nearness. "I just haven't met the right person."

"How do you know?" he pursued the conversation. "How do you know it wouldn't have taken one more look? Or one more kiss?"

"I don't think kissing someone proves anything," she rebuked.

"You don't think so?" He finished off his wine and put the glass down on the table.

She should have been warned by the tone of his voice. Alex always got *that* tone to his voice when he was trying to make a point. Then it was too late. He took her hands and pulled her forward, tugging gently until she was sitting up close to him.

"Kiss me, Carson."

"What?" she demanded, almost terrified as her heart gave a lurch then started racing.

"I want to prove a point here," he emphasized. "Kissing does mean something. No two people kiss alike, did you know that?" He began to trace her lips with a fingertip. "Tiny lines in the lips, the shape and size, even the muscles that control the strength of the kiss are different."

"Alex." She put her hands on his shoulders, feeling the texture of his shirt and the strength of the muscles beneath it. "I don't think—"

He bent close to her and touched his lips softly to a corner of her mouth. "Think of it as an experiment."

"Alex—" she protested weakly, when every fiber of her was aching to do as he requested, to feel his mouth on hers.

But as she had known it was, it was too late. He brought his mouth down on hers, taking her breath and her protests away. His arm swept behind her back and brought her up against his hard chest.

Carson was lost. For a long moment, she wasn't able to breathe or think. The world spun. Multicolored lights flashed in her brain. She wound her arms tightly around his neck.

His kiss changed, his lips alternately caressing and teasing hers. "You have a beautiful mouth, Carson," he whispered.

"Thanks," she replied thickly. "You, too."

She didn't resist, couldn't have said no if her life had depended on it. She felt like a rag doll in his arms while his kisses made her head spin.

There was a sound that permeated the black velvet that surrounded her. A loud, obnoxious sound that finally demanded to be heard.

A truck horn. Jackson and his four-wheel-drive truck.

"Well." Alex released her, sounding as unsteady as she felt. "I guess I proved my point."

Carson jumped up from the sofa. "You certainly proved Melanie's point," she told him, looking for her jacket and gloves.

"Melanie's point?"

"She says that we're too touchy-feely. You know. Hugging, kissing. Touching. She says friends don't do those things."

"I suppose—"

"That's Jackson," she told him above another blare from the truck. "Dad must have dispatched him over here."

"Carson." He stopped her, taking hold of her arm. "This does prove something."

"I know," she told him darkly. "It proves that we can't be friends when you're married, Alex. I have to go."

She picked up her jacket and ran down the stairs to the front door before he could say another word.

Alex sank down on the sofa and breathed deeply, trying to still his racing heart. "That's where you're wrong, friend of mine," he told the shadows where she had been a moment earlier. "That's where you're wrong."

Chapter Seven

Alex Langston had lived for five long years without Carson Myszkowski. It wasn't just his breakup with Paula that made him realize how much he'd missed her. But it was their breakup that made him realize that Carson was the woman he'd wanted the whole time. It was at that moment that he made the decision to come home, no matter what.

He'd left Seven Springs rather than have her family take him in out of pity. They were a large, gregarious family, and he'd been afraid of getting lost in the crowd. He'd also been afraid of Carson feeling sorry for him. He didn't think he could bear her pity.

It was harder to come back than he had guessed. The first few months, he'd wandered aimlessly around the country, from city to city, picking up work when he could and trying to understand a world that had taken from him everyone he'd ever loved.

He'd finally ended up joining the Army. The event changed his life. The discipline of the military life had given him purpose and put a name to the future he'd wanted. He'd learned quickly and advanced, staying one step ahead of any problems, learning to apply everything he'd learned to his future.

He'd met Morris Crane, and the two of them had started a software company in Morris's mother's basement. They'd worked long, hard hours to accomplish the first phase of their plan—to take their company public. During the celebration of that historic event, Alex had begun to formulate his return home.

He'd sold his part of the company to Morris but had stayed on as a consultant and software creator. He'd always liked the creative process better than the day-to-day workings of the corporation.

He'd contacted a construction company in Seven Springs that he'd remembered from his youth, and once the house restoration had begun, he'd taken a deep breath and had gone home.

The long hours had been devastating to his confidence. What if Carson didn't remember him? What if she wasn't the same person? Surely they had both changed. What if they didn't even like each other anymore?

He'd tried to imagine what sort of man she might be married to, but his mind had shied away from any clear picture. Carson was wonderful, warm and full of life and joy. It never occurred to him that she would still be alone. In his heart, he'd prayed that she had realized that she loved him, too. But his cynical mind rebuked him. What were the chances that Carson had waited for him?

When he'd lived in Seven Springs, with no family and no future, he'd known that Carson liked him and trusted him. He'd liked her and trusted her, too. And more. Recalling their hours together had kept him going through the worst of times. He wouldn't have done anything to hurt the delicate balance of friendship that existed between them.

Instinctively, he shied away from telling Carson his feelings when they were in school. He had nothing to offer her. No future to speak of. Even with her chopped-off hair and her crazy brothers, she was so far above him. *She* never made him feel that way, but he always knew it was true.

There was one night at the lake when he had wanted to kiss her and hold her so badly that he could have cried. He had managed to keep his hands to himself. But he had never looked at Carson again without wanting her.

After six years of thinking about it, he had finally kissed her.

It had been a surprise at first. He'd only been joking around with her, like they used to do. Daring her to go one step further. The touch of her lips on his had been a shock to his system. For one brief moment, he'd forgotten who he was holding in his arms and responded to her soft mouth and gentle sighs.

He had to admit that she was different than he'd imagined her. The reality had struck him forcefully, taking his breath away. When he'd first seen her, laughing and talking with her friends, he couldn't believe what a beautiful woman she'd become. Suddenly his visions of her changed. Carson was no longer a tall, gangly teenager with pretty hazel eyes and chopped-off hair.

She was a beautiful, elegant woman whose laughter captivated him. The short hair her mother had insisted on had grown long and silky. He'd wanted to touch it and managed to find a way to run his hands through it almost without thinking.

She *was* Carson, as he'd recalled her. Stubborn, argumentative, wanting to please. Yet very different. She hadn't married. She'd come back to Seven Springs after college to teach history. They were still close. But everything had altered between them.

He thought about it most of the night after she left, along with her words on their friendship. Maybe he was too "touchy-feely" as she'd claimed. She was probably right. And if he ever planned on marrying someone besides Carson Myszkowski, his new wife probably wouldn't have liked it. But that was never his intent.

He had wanted to see how she felt about marriage. Primarily about marrying *him*. He did plan on getting married and he did want Carson's cooperation in the scheme. He hadn't planned on her focusing so much on Paula. She was an area of his life that was best forgotten. He was grateful to her that she had reminded him of what was real and what he really wanted, but that was all. He loved Carson and he wanted to spend his life with her.

The next day, the temperature soared and by mid-afternoon, most of the snow had melted. Icicles formed from the roof and dripped in the sun. The trees shook off their white blankets and the roads cleared. Only the tops of the old mountains stayed frosty, glinting in the sun.

Alex had wanted to invite Carson back to his house to finish the decorating, but a problem with an old client, who was threatening to take his business elsewhere unless he saw Alex personally, was going to take him out of town for a few days.

He cursed the timing. He wanted to be with Carson to finish the house, and hopefully to find out if she felt the same way about him that he felt about her. It was so hard to say. Sometimes, he felt that she saw him as something more than a friend. Sometimes, she was distant.

When he'd kissed her, it had felt so right. It had been everything he'd ever imagined holding her in his arms. Then she'd stared at him as though he'd grown horns and made the pronouncement about not being friends after he was married. He was lost. He needed time to be with her, to get to know this woman who'd grown from the girl he'd left behind physically, but never in his heart.

But Morris had begged him for a few days. Alex had acquiesced. Maybe the separation would be good. Maybe he'd have a chance to sort through all of the conflicting data that was surging through his systems. Did she feel like he was more than a friend? Did she only see him as good old Alex?

Carson had offered to come by and take him to the airport to catch his plane. He'd accepted with alacrity. He wanted another chance to talk with her before he left. Maybe one more conversation would make a difference. Maybe something would begin to make sense. Maybe he could kiss her good-bye and know that she would think about him while he was gone.

Carson got out of her father's car slowly, the mud and slush crunching under her feet. She felt better when she saw that the wrecker had pulled Alex's Corvette out of the ditch. She did feel guilty even though she swore she wasn't going to.

Her father waved to Alex and they all watched as the wrecker took the Corvette away.

"Good to see you," Carson's father said. "Sorry about your car, Alex."

"Thanks, Mr. Myszkowski," Alex replied, feeling like a kid again.

"Good to have you back," her father said as he was backing out of the drive. "We'd like to have you over for dinner sometime."

Alex waved. "Thanks. I'd like that."

"Is it going to be okay?" Carson wondered as they climbed into her cold car that she'd left there the night before. She started the engine to let it warm up.

He stowed his single case in the backseat of the clean, gray Honda.

"Yeah." He glanced at his car. "It's dirty but intact. Dave's Garage is going to take a look at it for me while I'm gone. There's probably a lot of mud and grass in the rear axle."

"I'm really sorry," she apologized again, backing out of the driveway. "Although it wasn't totally my fault."

"Whatever damage is done, I'll let you pay for it just so that you feel better. Okay?"

She glanced at him before setting the car in motion on the road. "I don't feel *that* bad."

He laughed. "How bad do you feel?"

"Well—"

"Bad enough to come over and open the house for the painters tomorrow?"

"I think that would cover it." She nodded. "After all, you were driving too fast."

"But you did grab the steering wheel," he reminded her.

"I know." She shook her head. "I don't know what came over me."

He smiled evilly. "Nice Honda."

"All teachers don't drive Hondas," she relayed darkly. "And if you're implying that I panicked because I was riding in a sports car, you're wrong."

"Of course," he agreed, looking out the window at the mountains' profiles. "But if you could let the painters in and lock up when they leave, that would be a big help."

"I could do that," she relented. "How long are you going to be gone?"

"Probably only a day or two." He went on to explain to her about the man who was refusing to do business with anyone but him.

"What made you sell out your half of the company?" she wondered, her eyes on the road as she followed the interstate highway to the airport.

"It takes a lot of day-to-day stuff to keep it going. Morris always liked that part better than I did. I like how we started, writing the programs and working with the computers. I think it's going to work out for us except for this one account."

"You haven't been out of it very long," she observed. "You might miss all that stuff in New York."

"I might," he concurred, slanting an intent look her way. "Of course, then I'd be out of your hair again."

She looked back at him, realizing suddenly how much she would miss him if he left again. Her life had been fine without him all those years. She'd only realized since he'd come back that there had been something missing.

"Good," she teased pertly. "Then I'll move into your house. And you can pay me to live there and keep it up for you."

"For a history teacher, you're pretty mercenary." He

laughed, trying not to think about how much he hated to leave her again. In just a few days, she had managed to make herself indispensable to his life.

"I'm practical," she provided. "It's probably the only way I'm going to get out of my parents' house."

"Why don't you just move out?" he asked. "You're a big girl. The state does pay you to teach."

"I've tried." She sighed. "Every time I start to leave, my parents start having fits. I'll be so far away if I live in town, etc., etc. Your house would be perfect because it's so close."

He glanced at her as she parked the car. The light from the window traced a delicate shadow down her fragile jawline and caught in the highlights of her long hair. She'd worn it loose that day, and as she turned, strands of it fell across his hand that had been on the side of the seat between them. He let it slide through his fingers, reveling in the feelings that stirred inside of him.

The warm car smelled like her, a wonderful fragrance that reminded him of flowers in the meadow on a summer's day. He smiled and told her that she smelled good. Then he wanted to kick himself in the head when her face turned pink and she looked away. Melanie and her "touching" hypothesis had certainly put him in his place. He was going to have to rethink his approach for when he came back.

"I couldn't believe your father was asking me to come to your house and eat dinner," he remarked casually. "He was always throwing me out."

She glanced at him and her eyes were serious. "We aren't the same people anymore, Alex. It's strange, isn't it? Because sometimes, it seems like it was just yesterday. But it's different."

They closed the car doors and locked up. The wind was still brisk even though the sun was warm as they started walking toward the terminal building.

"You're still on that touching thing with Melanie, aren't you?" he guessed out loud, trying not to sound annoyed.

"Alex," she tried to explain. "Ever since I met you, I've been defending our relationship to everyone. All the kids at school thought we were a couple. My parents thought there was something more going on between us. Even your grandmother had a hard time believing we were just friends."

"And?" He wanted to hear it all before he left.

"And suddenly, what Melanie is saying makes sense. I have friends, Alex. Even some male friends. None of them would have kissed me like you did last night."

The doors swooshed open at their approach. He looked at the troubled lines on her face. She looked nervous and unhappy, not the way he wanted to leave her.

"We've been friends a long time," he tried to compensate.

"But you're going to be married," she responded.

"Someday," he reminded her. "I'm not married yet, Carson. There was nothing wrong with what happened between us last night."

He understood. She felt guilty. The kiss they'd shared had meant something special to her as well. Something that she thought they shouldn't be doing if he was going to marry someone else. That was something he loved about Carson. She was a woman of principle.

Yes! Maybe there was something there!

"It was just an experiment." He tried to make amends. "You were the one who said you couldn't tell anything about a person with a kiss."

He got into the ticket line and she waited while he checked in and they took his suitcase, wondering what it was that she *could* tell from that kiss.

And, mostly, wondering what *he* was able to glean from that experiment. What was going on behind those bright blue eyes? Was there a trace of mischief in their depths?

She wanted to ask him, but she felt strangely shy with him that afternoon. That kiss, and the long night she'd had to think about it, had altered their relationship forever.

Carson was in love with Alex. Maybe she had always loved him and just hadn't realized it. Whenever it had happened, that kiss had sealed her fate. It embarrassed her to think that she was in love with him but that he might not love her. She thought about all the things that she had confided to him and they made her cringe.

"I still have twenty minutes before the plane boards," he told her when he'd finished. "Have a cup of coffee with me."

She wanted to say no. She didn't want to look at him, standing in the bright airport terminal, handsome in his black suit and crisp white shirt. He didn't look like Alex. Not *her* Alex. He looked like the stranger who she had kissed last night. The stranger who she wanted to kiss again. The man she loved.

Then he smiled down at her, and despite everything, he was still Alex. Alex who'd climbed her trellis. Alex who'd jumped his motorcycle across Clingman's

Gorge on a bet. Alex who'd listened while she cried out her woes on the way home from school.

"Okay," she decided a little mutinously, turning from him and heading for the coffee shop in the terminal.

He frowned. "You don't have to sound like I just asked you to have a tooth pulled."

She didn't answer. He followed her to the coffee shop and sat in a corner, across the tiny table from her. There was so much he wanted to say to her. When had he become so tongue-tied with her?

The waitress brought them both a cup of coffee then left them alone. The coffee shop was mostly deserted between flights. The sound of a soap opera blared from the back of the counter.

"So, what's up?" he asked nervously, scared that he'd finally pushed their friendship too far last night and that she wasn't ready for anything else.

He could see her worrying her lip, a sure sign that she was working up to saying something. Carson always thought out what she was going to say before she blasted the skin from his bones.

"Alex," she blurted out suddenly, "how did you know that you loved Paula?"

"What?" he stalled, sipping his coffee, wondering what had prompted that question and how he should answer it.

"How did you know?" she repeated. "Did you know her a long time? Did you have some special feeling that you never had for anyone else? Are you going to see her while you're gone?"

She hadn't meant to ask the last, but the question had gnawed at her since he'd called and asked her to take him to the airport. He was probably going to see her, she reasoned, watching the cream disappear into her coffee. It might even be the reason he was going to New York. He might have lied to her about the whole business excuse.

Alex drew in a deep breath, teetering between uncertainty and elation that she might be jealous. She *sounded* jealous. Was it possible that Carson was jealous? Did she hate the idea that he might be going to see Paula? Did she feel something for him besides friendship?

He looked at her, with her head bent over her coffee cup, pretending an interest in the steaming brown liquid that was unwarranted. He touched her hand, and she jumped, then looked up at him.

"Carson, what's really bothering you?"

"I told you," she answered truthfully. "I'm worried about you. About how you feel about Paula and if you're really ready for another relationship. I think you should think it over very carefully. You don't want to make another mistake."

"I'm not going to see Paula," he assured her confidently. "I'm going to help Morris with a difficult but important client. We're going to talk business. Then I'm coming home. I know what I want, Carson."

Carson felt her heart jump in excitement then plunge in despair. "Sorry," she murmured. "I worry too much. I'll take a hard look at every single, eligible woman I can think of while you're gone."

"That's great," he returned in a less-than-enthusiastic voice. Was it too late to go back on what he'd told her and tell her that he wasn't interested in meeting other women? "I just want to find someone who can love me for myself."

"Exactly," she agreed wholeheartedly. "If I loved you—"

Alex's coffee cup stopped abruptly on its return trip to the saucer.

"I mean, theoretically," she tried to correct with a steadily reddening face. "If I loved you or . . . or anyone, I would love you or . . . or anyone else for themselves. You have a lot to offer someone, Alex."

Alex wasn't sure his internal organs could take much more of the roller-coaster ride he'd put them through since he'd come home. His heart stopped then bumped haltingly to its normal beat again.

"So, one way or another, this should decide our future," he concluded with a deep breath, going quickly past her declaration.

Carson worried her lower lip again then glanced up at him. "*Our* future?" she questioned. She pushed her hair back behind one ear with a quick motion.

His gaze narrowed on hers, and her eyes skittered away from that questioning intensity. "Our future," he repeated, lost for words. "You know, like everyone's future. The future of the whole planet." *Lame.* He winced at his own words. *Very lame.*

"Oh." She stood up suddenly, upsetting the tiny table and the two cups. "I have to go."

The waitress jumped up from behind the counter, thinking she had missed something, and scurried over to them.

"I should go," he rationalized, looking at his watch.

"I know," she said, smiling shakily up at him, wanting to reach out to those broad shoulders and hold on to him. "I'll walk you down the concourse."

It was just because he'd been gone so long, she explained to herself, walking quietly beside him. It was just because they were so close and she had missed him so much. It was just because of that kiss and that whole stupid experiment. And wasn't it just like Alex to upset all her notions about the world, then calmly brush it aside as some experiment?

They walked through the metal detectors without incident and silently began the long walk down the green carpeted corridor that led to the loading area for the planes.

"I left the paint samples for each room taped to a spot near the light switches where you walk in," he said as the silence lengthened and he needed to speak. It was either talk about something mundane or beg her to come with him and tell her that he couldn't bear to leave her again.

"I can take care of that," she assured him, watching the way their hands moved as they walked. So close to one another, yet never touching.

"There might be a few phone calls about furniture," he added. "Possibly even a delivery, although I don't expect one."

"Okay," she answered, casually letting her hand swing close enough to his that their knuckles brushed. "Alex?"

"Carson?"

They laughed as his hand captured hers. They'd reached the end of the concourse and the boarding sign was out for his plane.

"I—I didn't mean to pry," she said, trying to apologize. Whether or not he saw his ex-girlfriend was his business.

"That's okay," he said, feeling his throat tighten as he looked at her, wondering if he could let go of her hand and get on the plane.

"Well, I guess you should go before they leave you," she commented, glancing at the plane that waited outside the tall windows on the steaming tarmac.

He nodded, not trusting himself to speak and managed to let go of her hand.

"Have a good flight." She smiled and reached up, putting her arms around him without thinking, hugging him tightly to her. "Don't wait so long to come back this time."

"I won't," he whispered, devastated by the feel of her against him.

She moved her head back and looked at him. There were tears in her eyes and her lips were trembling.

No power on earth could have stopped him from kissing her. Without stopping to think or question what he was feeling, he brought his mouth down on hers.

She welcomed him, parting her lips beneath his, winding herself closer until they were fused together by the raw heat of their emotions.

"Excuse me," the flight attendant at the gate interrupted, "but if this is your plane-"

"Alex!" she whispered, shaken as they parted, touching her mouth with a worried hand.

"Carson, I—" he began, touching her face. He shook his head, words failing him, and turned to show his ticket to the attendant. "I'll be back as soon as I can," he managed in a strangled voice.

She smiled and waved, not trusting her voice as she wiped away silent tears that rolled down her face. She stood and watched as the plane doors were closed and the plane started to move down the runway, standing for long minutes after it had disappeared from sight before she realized that he was gone and that she should leave as well.

What was happening between them? she wondered as she walked back out to her car. How was it possible, that after all those years, she was suddenly, desperately in love with Alex?

She knew that she would miss him while he was gone, but in a way she was glad that he was away for a few days. She needed time to think about everything, to put their relationship back into its proper perspective. Something she had been trying to accomplish since he'd come back home.

He might come not back again from New York, a small, dark voice, that refused to keep silent, whispered to her. *He might be gone for good this time.* She might never see him again and he would never know that she loved him.

Or Alex might decide that he had to come back. Once he'd come home to Seven Springs, and they'd met again after all those years, he might have realized that he loved someone he'd known a lot longer.

He might love you, a little angel voice whispered in golden tones. *Alex Langston might love you, Carson Myszkowski.*

A random image of the two of them in his grandmother's house wandered through her mind and intoxicated her with its devastating presence.

But what if that didn't happen? She frowned, doubting the joy that the image had generated. What if she had to go on living as his friend, watching while he and his wife had children and shared their lives? What if she had to teach history to their son or daughter?

The concept squirmed inside of her like a terrible writhing snake fueled by jealousy and longing.

Driving home slowly and carefully from the airport, Carson didn't even realize that she had gone back to Alex's house until she stopped the car and looked up.

The key was in her pocket and the painters wouldn't be coming until the next day.

She just wanted to walk through the house and remember it as it had been when his grandmother was still alive, she told herself, getting out of the car. She would look at the colors they'd chosen again to make sure they were right.

Once she was inside, though, she admitted to herself that she wanted to look at those things he'd left behind. Those personal things that made the place belong to him.

She wandered absently through the rooms, picking up personal items that she'd noticed when she'd been there but hadn't wanted to take the time to look at. She'd accused him of snooping into her life; she hadn't wanted to appear to do so in his.

She looked in his office. He'd won awards for his software designs even though the categories and the recognition weren't anything she understood. Basically, she was computer illiterate besides turning on a machine in the computer lab at school. One of her students had showed her how to get on the Internet and find historical data, but while she'd been grateful, she also couldn't recall how to do it when she'd tried on her own.

In his bedroom, she looked at the little things that made it belong to Alex. With his marked love of blue, he owned three blue sweaters and a dozen blue shirts. She smiled at his mixed-match pairs of alternate blue socks in a basket near the bathroom.

Her arm brushed against a midnight-blue bathrobe,

soft and plush, hanging on a hook on the bathroom door. She put her hand on it, then glancing around, put her arms into the enormous sleeves and pulled it around her. It smelled like him, like his aftershave, and it swallowed her, hanging down over her feet as she wrapped the folds closer.

What would he think? she wondered, looking at herself in the huge bathroom mirror over the vanity and sinks. What would he say if he walked into the room that minute and she was wearing his robe?

What would he say if he knew that she thought of him as more than just a friend? Melanie had been right. She hated to realize that her friend had seen it before she had but it was true.

Alex was special. He had always been special to her. He'd found a place in her heart years before he'd ever left. Even when he was actually gone, roaming around the world, he'd stayed there inside of her. Maybe she'd always loved him. Maybe it had waited until he'd come back for her to see it.

Was that what his grandmother had seen, all those years ago, when she saw them together? Was that why her parents had been so afraid for her to go out with him so often, because they saw through the lie she had told herself about their relationship?

She rested her cheek against the soft material of the robe and closed her eyes, remembering what it had been like to be in his arms. He had kissed her until she couldn't think to struggle, didn't want him to stop. Yet he had dismissed it as an experiment, as just a way of proving his point about kisses being different.

What had he said? she mused, touching her lips with her fingers, feeling them tingle as they had when he'd kissed her. That the tiny lines in the lips and the strength of the muscles all combined to make the kiss different.

She sighed and wondered if he had felt anything. Was it all a joke to him? Was the only real love he'd felt for Paula?

And what about when he'd kissed her good-bye at the airport? That had felt real. He hadn't even attempted to shrug it off as part of the experiment.

Did Alex feel something for her?

Chapter Eight

T he phone rang, and her eyes flew open. She dropped the heavy robe on the cool tile floor and raced to find the sound, thinking that it might be the painters.

Before she could reach Alex's office, the call had already been answered. She stood and waited, looking out of the windows over the valley, while the fax came through.

If it was something important, she thought, she could always call Alex. He'd given her the name and number of the hotel where he was staying in New York.

When the machine signaled that the message was finished, she picked up the sheet and scanned it quickly. It might be important, she argued with herself about reading Alex's mail.

To: Alex
From: Paula
Subject: Reuniting

Morris told me about your trip to the city! I've canceled everything, darling, so that when you leave NY, I'll be beside you on the plane. I hope the house is ready. I can't wait to see it. And Severed Springs. Love you!

Carson stood in Alex's office, looking at the paper in her hands. She hoped that if she read it enough times, it would change. But it stayed the same. Paula was coming back with Alex.

Suddenly nothing made sense, and yet everything was clear. Melanie had been right! Oh, how right she had been!

Carson knew she couldn't stand the idea of Paula being there in the house with Alex. Not because she was selfish or indifferent. Because *she* wanted to be there. All that time, she had loved him and had never realized it. Now it was too late!

"So, let's recap," Melanie said as they rushed from their car to the mall on Wednesday through icy mountain winds.

"Alex is coming back with Paula, his ex-girlfriend," Carson explained briefly. "She faxed him the message after he'd left for New York."

"And suddenly, you realize that you do love him after all," Melanie finished on a triumphant note. "I don't want to say I told you so but I did tell you so."

Carson nodded miserably. "And I know that he loves Paula even though he said that they were through. He only broke up with her because she wasn't ready to settle down."

"Does he feel anything for you?" Melanie wondered, shivering as the warmth of the mall's interior hit them.

"I don't know," Carson responded. "He kissed me before he left. At the airport, when it wasn't part of the experiment."

"What experiment?" Melanie demanded, narrowing her eyes.

Carson explained about what had happened the night before he left. "But he said it was an experiment to make me understand that a kiss could change your mind about someone."

Melanie rolled her eyes. "That sounds like a dumb guy-thing to me. If he was experimenting with anyone, it was probably with himself! Maybe he has his doubts, too. Maybe he's not sure if he just wants to be your friend now."

"I don't think so," Carson replied wistfully. "I think he feels something for me, but I don't think he loves me. Not like Paula."

They both sighed heavily as they walked toward the bookstore where Melanie was picking up a gift.

"There might be a way to find out," Melanie suggested slowly as the idea rolled through her brain with the inexorable motion of a freight train.

"Melanie—"

"It's just an idea! If you don't like it, you can wallow in your pain and forget about it," her friend defended the as-yet-unheard idea.

Normally, Carson didn't ask when she heard Melanie begin to come up with one of her crazy ideas. But she was desperate and insane at the idea of seeing Alex get off the plane with Paula beside him, ready to take over his house.

"What?" Carson asked hesitantly as they paused in the doorway under the Stephen King poster.

Melanie's face was thoughtful as she began to work out her plan. "Either way, you come off looking better."

"Better than what?" Carson muttered, trailing behind her friend into the store.

After a few purchases for Melanie's nephew, they ended up in the ice cream shop sitting across from each other at a pink-and-green striped table.

"So, you're suggesting that I pretend to have suddenly found someone?" Carson asked, trying to understand the intricacies of the plan.

"I'm suggesting that you either find out that he does care for you, or you salvage your pride in case he has any idea that you feel something else for him."

Carson shook her head. "And how do you suggest I do that?"

"I have it all worked out!" Melanie smiled and patted Carson's shoulder.

"It might be a mistake if he does feel something for me," Carson said as she scooped up some hot fudge with her spoon. "It could end everything right there."

Melanie made a face at her. "No man was ever put off by competition! It's not in their nature. They always want something more because they can't have it. Especially a woman! If he does care for you, he's not going to back down because of a little competition. It'll bring him right up to snuff, as my old granny used to say."

Carson still felt a little of that initial hurt and confusion racing through her system. She wasn't sure about Melanie's idea, but she did know that a "love interest" would at least keep Alex at a distance until she could get through the whole thing.

If he hugged her again or wanted to try any more experimental kissing, she thought that she might fall apart.

"So?"

"What do you have in mind, Melanie?"

Melanie grinned. "All right. I've got a plan. Trust me. This will work."

"What will work?" Carson asked, trying to show her enthusiasm. "I haven't heard any details yet."

"We're going to show Alex that you are desirable and other men want you, so if he's interested at all, he better get his act together! And once we've shown him, then we can plan a great wedding. Either for Alex and Paula or for you and Alex."

Carson winced. "What am I going to show him? I don't have a secret past, and I've already told him that I'm not involved with anyone."

"He's going to be gone for a few days," Melanie improvised. "Plenty of time for an enterprising young man to sweep you off your feet."

Carson looked at her friend blankly. "Who?"

Melanie preened in her moment of absolute brilliance. "My brother, Sam, is coming home for two weeks. He'll be in later tonight. Tomorrow when you meet him, the two of you will fall hopelessly in love, and by the time Alex comes back, there won't be a person in town who doesn't know about it!"

"What about Sam, Melanie?" Carson doubted. "I'm not sure he'll want to spend his time pretending to be my dearest love!"

She shrugged. "He's going to be staying with Mom and Dad for a few days. Next weekend, he's going to

Rose Creek. It won't hurt him to be seen with you a few times. He owes me a favor."

"That's all it'll take," Carson acknowledged miserably, knowing that she and Sam would be an item before anyone bothered to ask her what was going on.

"To make the plan work?" Melanie demanded.

"To ruin my life!"

"You're so negative!"

"I don't believe in playing games." Carson told her. "It goes against my nature."

"So, you'd rather suffer?" Melanie questioned without sympathy. "You'd rather let someone else have the man you love?"

Carson squirmed uneasily. What if Melanie was right? "If he does care about me, and he finds out—"

"He won't find out," Melanie finished. "If there's nothing between the two of you, he and Paula will be married, and Sam will fade out. If there is something between you, and he tells you how he feels, Sam will fade out. Either way, you'll feel better."

"I don't know what to say." Carson argued with her conscience for a few minutes.

"Never mind." Melanie drew her friend closer. "It's only a matter of timing and planning. This is what we'll do . . ."

The next morning when Tom Mace and Mary Lou Bennet were drinking coffee at the coffee shop, they saw a black BMW pull up in front of the middle school and drop off its passenger.

"That's Carson Myszkowski," Mary Lou said the other woman's name with less than enthusiasm. "Her hair looks awful this morning."

"Who's that she's with?" Tom wondered.

"Is that . . . yes, that's Sam Marshall. He's Melanie Tyne's brother. I thought he was living in Chicago or somewhere." Mary Lou jockeyed for a better look at the car and its passengers.

"He might be," Tom observed as he watched the pair embrace, "but he's here with Carson right now."

"Is that all right?" Sam asked with a brilliant smile after he'd kissed Carson with a flourish.

"That's great, Sam. Thanks."

"I'll pick you up this afternoon?"

"This afternoon," Carson agreed, gritting her teeth.

She walked into the school building, finally realizing why it was that Melanie had offered her brother for her knight-errant.

Sam had just been dumped by a long-term girl-friend, and he wanted to talk about it. To anyone. Nonstop. If she didn't know better, Carson might have thought Melanie's parents had planned the whole thing just to get rid of him while he was staying there until he went to Rose Creek.

She'd gone by Alex's house, and Dave had been there, dropping off the Corvette. He'd seen the flashy BMW and noticed the hug she'd bestowed on its occupant before she went to open the door of the house for the painters.

It wouldn't take long. The grapevine was well planted in Seven Springs.

The school day was too long for her. Half of the day, she spent wishing that it was Alex in his old Corvette that was meeting her after school. The other half, she spent angry at herself for not taking the chance and telling him how she felt about him.

What did she stand to lose? Her pride would be

demolished if he looked at her and told her that he'd never felt that way about her. Her heart would be broken in about a hundred thousand pieces. But if he married another woman, there was no chance for them. Her heart would be broken and she would have to learn to live without him.

Everything had become so complicated. She sighed. She had agreed to pretend to be in love with someone else so that Alex might decide that he was in love with her. The whole thing was impossible! She almost decided against going through with the plot. She knew Alex. He wasn't a game-player. If she came right out and told him the truth, what was the worst that could happen? Once they got through the initial awkwardness of the situation, everything would be fine between them. One way or another.

But it was like a snowball rolling downhill.

By the time she got home, her mother was asking her about the good-looking man in the BMW. When she admitted that it was Melanie's brother, her father smiled.

"Finally over that fascination with Alex Langston, huh?"

"We're only friends!" She defended from habit only to bite her tongue as the words came out of her mouth. Hopefully, she would have to get over that excuse!

Her mother looked at her with her left eyebrow raised, and Carson knew they were in for a long talk.

"I have to go back out and lock up Alex's house." She evaded that talk, at least for the moment.

"He called here for you today," her mother told her, taking down a jar of green beans that she'd canned last summer.

"Alex?" Carson asked, her heart beating a rapid tattoo.

Her mother nodded. "He wants you to pick him up at the airport tomorrow evening. He'll be on the six-thirty flight from Atlanta."

Tomorrow!

"He must have finished up faster than he thought," she said out loud, looking at her gloved hands and smiling.

"What's wrong, Carsy?" her mother asked quietly. "Is it Alex?"

"It's nothing," she replied as naturally as possible. "I have to go. Don't wait up for me. I'll be at Melanie's."

Alex was coming home tomorrow! Her heart sang with it. Yet the news weighed heavily on her mind.

Could she go through with the charade they'd planned for that weekend? What if Alex did feel something for her and he realized it while he was gone? Did she want to hurt him that way? To make him think she was infatuated with another man?

And still, maybe she was wrong. She didn't know if she had enough courage to walk up to Alex and tell him that she thought she was in love with him. All the time they'd spent together, all the things they'd done. Even though she knew him so well, she didn't know if she could find the words. She imagined herself looking into his eyes and saying, "I love you, Alex" and him laughing and hugging her and saying, "I love you, too, Carson. Let's talk about my honeymoon with Paula."

Melanie had been right about the way she felt about Alex. She might be right about how to handle the situation. Wouldn't it be much easier if Alex was jealous of Sam and came right out and told her that he loved her? Maybe having Sam around for that weekend would afford her a chance to find out how Alex really felt about her without that terrible risk to her pride.

Of course, they were assuming that Alex would go to Rose Creek with the Historical Society. If he decided to stay home for the weekend, he would hear all the rumors and the innuendoes, but he wouldn't see Carson and Sam together.

Carson grimaced. All that would happen would be that she would have to spend a whole weekend listening to Sam tell her about how beautiful and wonderful his ex-girlfriend was and how much he wanted her back.

Despite Melanie's assurances that everything would work out, Carson spent most of that night awake and all of the next day at school jumping whenever anyone said her name.

Sam took her to school again and picked her up afterward. By that time, of course, everyone was watching for them, and people were clamoring for information about her newest "friend." Sam was handsome and he was from out of town. He was perfect grist for the rumor mill that was grinding at full speed in Seven Springs.

"What happened to Alex Langston?" Tom Mace asked her between classes in the teacher's lounge.

"He's out of town," she told him without thinking.

He let out a long, low whistle. "Playing 'em close to the edge, aren't you, Carson? While the cat's away . . ."

"Never mind." She picked up her apple and walked out of the lounge.

"I brought something to show you," Sam told her as she climbed into his car after school.

"Oh! What?" she asked, hoping it would be something that would take his mind off of his girlfriend.

He handed her a picture. "It's all I have left of her," he said glumly.

The woman with the heavy makeup and the brassy blond hair smiled out at her with a white, toothy smile.

"I'm sure it will work out between you," Carson soothed, handing the picture back to him.

"You might as well keep it." He sighed. "It won't do me any good."

Carson sighed and tucked the picture under the seat when she thought he wasn't looking. They drove out to Alex's house again where the painters were finishing up for the day.

"Only one more room," A. J. Walters told her with a tobacco-stained grin. "We should be finished tomorrow."

"Alex will be back tonight," she informed him. "He'll probably want to look everything over."

"Sure!" He waved. "See you!"

Carson looked wistfully at the house, wanting to go inside and look around yet needing not to feel so sentimental if she were going to pick up Alex and Paula that evening and pretend to be in love with Sam.

Looking back over the time they'd spent there made her want to cry. How many secrets had they shared there while his grandmother was in the kitchen making cookies? How many nights had she sneaked out of her house and met him there and they had made plans to leave Seven Springs and never come back?

"Why couldn't you have fallen in love with me,

Alex?" she asked the empty room as she locked the door and climbed back into Sam's warm car.

"Want me to go out with you and pick Alex up tonight?" he asked when they started back down the road to her home.

"No," she replied flatly. "I want to see him alone."

"He won't be alone, will he? Didn't you say he'd have his fiancé with him? Melanie didn't think that was such a great idea," he reminded her briefly. "Maybe you should reconsider."

"I want to talk to him. Alone, if there's an opportunity, Sam." She shook her head and threaded her fingers back through her hair. "He might be alone, after he's thought it over. He might have come to the same conclusion that I did. I don't want to hurt him that way."

Sam pulled into her driveway and waved to Jackson who was walking into the house. The two men had been on the Whitmore football team together.

"You know, Carson," he began, turning toward her and lightly touching her arm, "I think we might be missing something here."

"Something like what?" she asked, unhappy and bewildered.

"Something like what's happening between us."

Oh, great! She felt like groaning. All she needed was for Sam to think she seemed like a good rebound from his girlfriend.

"There's nothing happening here . . . between us, anyway," she told him bluntly. "I know you're unhappy, Sam, but things will get better for you. Just hang in there."

"It's more than that, Carson." He smiled at her sadly. "I won't say anything else until you talk with

Alex. Maybe when you see him again, you'll realize. The two of us could be good together."

"Good night, Sam," she said finally. "I'll see you tomorrow."

"Good night, Carson," he said a little pathetically.

"I do appreciate your help," she relented, seeing his sad face.

"My pleasure." He brightened.

Carson slammed into the house, ripped off her coat and gloves, then stormed upstairs to her room. It took less than a minute to get Melanie on the phone and before her friend could speak, Carson blasted her for letting her use Sam in his delicate frame of mind.

"It's good for him," Melanie assured her, balancing a baby in one arm and a bowl of salad in the other while her husband held the phone to her ear.

"Good for him?" Carson wondered. "He's beginning to think he's really in love with me, Melanie."

There was silence on the other end of the line, then she heard Melanie ask her husband to take the baby.

"It's going to be over soon," Melanie finally replied when her children were being fed. Her husband was shaking his head over the whole thing but she ignored him.

"I hope you're right." Carson drew a deep breath and prayed for calm.

"Once Alex gets back tonight and finds out about Sam, he'll want to be at Rose Creek over the weekend. The two of you play it up, and by Sunday night, you and I will be talking about where to register you for your wedding gifts."

"Unless he really does love Paula," Carson reminded her. "Or he hears about this thing with Sam and it ruins everything."

Melanie put a bowl of potatoes on the table. "We'll have to hope for the best, Carson. I've got my money on you."

Carson was tired and dispirited. She sat down on her bed and closed her eyes. "I hope so. I know I'm going to hate telling Alex tonight that Sam and I are suddenly in love, even if Paula is standing right next to him."

"Are you taking Sam with you?" Melanie wondered.

"No," Carson whispered as someone knocked on her door. "I need to see him alone. Well, if I have the chance to see him alone. I'm not telling him anything about Sam if *she's* not with him."

"Carson," Melanie warned, "he's going to be there with Paula! She's not going to let you steal him out from under her!"

Carson cut her off as the knock came louder the second time. "Got to go, Mel. I'll call you when I get home tonight and tell you what he says."

"Carson?"

Carson hung up the phone and opened her bedroom door. "Lee!" She hugged her older brother. "What are you doing here?"

"I let Riley talk me into being part of this Rose Creek thing. They were short on help for the weekend."

"I'm so glad to see you!" She hugged him again.

"What's up, Carson? Mom says you've been running around with Alex Langston again."

Her tall, older brother with his serious brown eyes walked into her room and closed the door and that was it. It only took her a minute to tell him everything, and the relief of not holding it inside was welcome. The frown on Lee's handsome face wasn't.

"Carson," he started, trying to put his feelings into words. "If Alex does have feelings for you, and I'm not saying that he does because he seems to be pretty taken with this other woman, won't you be defeating your own chances? He doesn't know how you feel about him. If you show up with Sam, what will make Alex tell you how he feels any more than you can tell him right now? If Maggie hadn't allowed for me being blind and helped me out a little, we wouldn't be married."

Carson smiled weakly. "Melanie thought I could salvage my pride, if nothing else."

"Not if he walks away because he doesn't think you love him," Lee stated plainly. "Sometimes you have to put your pride on the line, Carsy. You might have to take a chance on being the first one to say it."

"I know you're right, Lee. I just don't know how to tell him how I feel. We really were only friends. Until now."

He considered it for a minute then looked up at her, a smile in his eyes. "I think you should try, honey. No matter how it comes out, you'll be glad."

She glanced up at him. "Maybe this isn't the best answer."

"No doubt about that," Lee agreed heartily.

"And maybe I should try to tell him," she finished, bolstering her courage with her brother's assurances. He had never steered her wrong. "Would you come with me to tell him?"

Lee stood up from the chair in the corner of her room. "I'm not going there, Carsy. Some things you have to do for yourself. I hope it works out for you.

I always thought you and Alex would be good to-gether. I'd like to live long enough to see you settled."

Carson laughed. "It's like I was telling Melanie the other day about old married people. You all want to see other people married, too."

"I think that'll do," he stopped her before he heard any more. "Mom wanted me to bring you downstairs for dinner. I've done more than my duty."

"I couldn't eat," she said, then glanced at her watch. "And I have to get ready to go to the airport."

"Good luck, Carson. If you need me, I'll be here. This is no time to be a coward. You have to be brave to be in love."

"Thanks, Lee."

When her brother was gone, Carson stripped off her serviceable slacks and blouse and vest then stood under the shower for a short time.

If she was going to go through with her plan to lay it all out for Alex, she was going to look her best. It wouldn't make her feel any better about being re-jected, but she would know that she would have given it her best shot.

It was strange, the idea of dressing up for Alex. Their friendship had included so many times when she'd worn dirty jeans and hadn't bothered about her hair. It was a new experience to wonder what he thought about how his old friend looked.

Not that she adhered to Melanie's principles that people shouldn't be friends and lovers. She had al-ready spent long moments entertaining the thought of being in Alex's arms. She knew him well, even after so many years apart, but kissing him, touching him, even hearing him talk about admiring her legs, had brought a new dimension to their relationship.

Dress for success, all the fashion magazines said. In this case, success would be Alex not being able to keep away from her, breaking down and confessing that he loved her. Otherwise the weekend dragged out before her like an invitation to a plague.

She had two dresses in her closet that she considered indecent. One was a sequined blue party dress that she'd worn two years before for New Year's Eve.

That would have to be for the honeymoon, she judged, holding it against her in the long mirror.

The second was a burgundy Japanese silk that looked more like a slip than a dress. She'd bought it half-price after Christmas, not sure where or when she would wear such a thing. It took her usual staid image of a schoolteacher and tossed it out the window. If someone from the school board saw her wearing it, she would hate to think of the repercussions.

She pulled it on quickly, not giving herself a chance for second thoughts or self-doubt. Now wasn't the time to hide her light, she determined, looking at the dress as it clung in all the right places.

She brushed her hair until it gleamed then left it free to fall over her bare shoulders. She wore a little more makeup than she usually allowed herself and pulled on pantyhose and high heels that made her legs look as though they went on forever. She studied herself in the mirror. If Alex thought her legs looked good in the red shorts, he wasn't going to be able to keep his eyes off of her!

Her feet were going to ache by the time she walked through the airport. She pulled on her heavy knee-length wool coat. Hopefully, the look on Alex's face would be worth it.

It was obvious from the look on her family's faces

that Lee had spilled it all to them as quickly as he'd gone downstairs.

"I'm going to the airport to get Alex," she told them as she walked past the table to the door. "I'll be back later."

"Be careful, Carsy," her father warned in unusually gruff tones.

"I will be," she promised.

"Carson—" her mother began, then bit her lip. "The roads might be slippery tonight."

"I'll be careful, Mom."

The roads were dry, of course. The sun had melted almost all the ice and snow away even from the shadows of the mountains where it clung in the frozen breezes.

Her parents were worried, and so was Lee. She couldn't honestly say that she wasn't worried. She could only hope her strategy would bring about a quick end to her relationship with Sam.

Her car felt as though it flew toward the airport. Too soon for her mind, but not soon enough for her heart. Words that expressed her love for him came and were rejected as she tried desperately to decide what she would say to him.

She had taken off her coat in the warmth of the airport terminal's heating system, and she was waiting breathlessly at the gate for Alex's face as the crowd of passengers disembarked.

When she saw him, her heart lurched in her chest. Her face suffused with heat. Anything that she had planned to say, flew out of her mind. Her old friend Alex was back home. Yet he was a stranger to her. He was so handsome in his dark suit, his black hair in place and his caramel eyes sweeping the crowd.

It made her breath come a little faster to know that he was looking for her, and when their gazes locked, Carson waved, smiling until her face hurt.

Alex smiled back and waved to her. She thought he looked tired, his eyes a little darker. Maybe he was worried, she considered. Maybe he'd been confused as well and had hated to leave her. Maybe he was as unsure as she felt after their last moments at the airport before he'd left.

"Look, there she is!" Melanie's voice carried through the crowd as she towed Sam behind her to reach Carson's side.

"What are you doing here?" Carson demanded. "I told you I wanted to see him alone."

"Dressed like that?" Melanie queried. "We both know where this would've ended."

Sam stepped forward and did his duty, putting his arm around Carson's shoulders. He was a tall, handsome man, normally self-assured and confident of his life and his emotions. It showed on him in the way he dressed and carried himself.

That was the face that Alex saw as he reached Carson's side. The man looked and dressed like a lawyer. His clothes were expensive and his hold on Carson was possessive.

Alex gritted his teeth and the knuckles on the hand that held his travel bag turned white. Despite the fact that he had just negotiated a multimillion-dollar contract, he began to feel like he'd lost everything.

"Alex?" A honeyed voice floated with his name to reach him. "Are you going to introduce me to your friends?"

Alex turned to the stunning blond and smiled. "Of course. Paula, this is my good friend, Carson Myszkowski. Carson, this is Paula Jones."

Chapter Nine

Paula was everything that Carson had been terrified that she would be. Tall, thin, well-dressed, and beautiful. She had the kind of poise and self-assurance that came with knowing that the whole world was looking at you. And they knew that you were gorgeous.

"Hello, Carson!" Paula laid her fingers in the palm of Carson's hand. They were cool to the touch. Her nails were long and beautifully manicured.

Alex stared at Carson for a long moment. Carson stared back, wanting nothing more than to run out of the airport and into the night, screaming.

"Hello, Alex," Melanie greeted him, trying to break their awkward, silent stare.

"Hello, Melanie," Alex responded but didn't take his eyes off of Carson.

Carson couldn't look away. Sam was at her side, but he might have been on the moon for all she cared. Alex looked tired and upset. She wanted to hold him

149

close and whisper that everything was going to be all right.

"This is my brother, Sam," Melanie introduced the two men. "He was a few years ahead of us so you two probably never met."

Alex shook hands with Sam, and the two men's gazes locked.

"Sam."

"Alex."

"Hi! I'm Melanie Tyne," Melanie introduced herself to Paula awkwardly. "We're here to pick up a few of the people from the Stone Mountain Historical Society from Georgia for the Rose Creek exhibit this weekend." She laughed nervously. "Then Sam saw Carson, and well, it's been hard to keep them apart since he got back Thursday."

"I see," Alex returned simply.

"You must be exhausted." Carson finally found her voice, prying herself away from Sam's overardent hold. "The car's this way." She couldn't stand there any longer. Her heart felt like someone was trying to pry it out of her chest. Maybe her pride was intact but it was little consolation.

"I guess we'll see you later," Melanie inserted.

"Be careful, angel," Sam murmured, grabbing hold of Carson as she would have walked away and kissing her upturned lips.

"I'll call you," Carson promised no one in particular.

" 'Bye," Paula called out with a lilting wave. "Nice to meet you!"

It was worse, far worse than anything she could have imagined. Maybe Lee had been right. Maybe she should have been able to tell Alex how she felt, but there hadn't been time, and now it was too late.

She walked quickly to catch up with Alex and Paula who had picked up their bags and were heading for the door. So much for her dress, she considered, pulling her coat back around herself before she braved the cold night air.

"Thanks for coming to get us," Alex said, his breath frosty as they walked through the parking deck.

She nodded miserably. "Did everything go well?"

"Better than well, didn't it, darling?" Paula replied for him, linking her arm through his and looking up lovingly into his face.

He glanced at her. "Everything went fine, Carson."

What have you been doing while I was gone? he wanted to demand. *I was gone five years and you didn't meet anyone. Then in two days, you meet Mr. Right? How could you?*

He had made it plain to Paula when she had tracked him down in New York. He was in love with Carson. There was no going back. She had insisted on coming back with him to Seven Springs anyway. As his friend. She wanted to see his house, she insisted. She wanted to meet his friends.

"Good! Good! That's very, uh, good."

"Oh, he's so modest," Paula told her. "He closed a huge account! Snatched it right out from under the noses of those guys from LA who thought they could take it!"

"That's wonderful," Carson enthused, realizing that she'd been wrong in thinking that Alex might feel something for her. Paula was beautiful. Exciting. Everything that Carson had never been and would never be. Paula looked like a model. Carson looked like a schoolteacher.

And she loved him, too, she recalled with something like illness clenching her stomach. Just that she didn't want to settle down. It looked like she had changed her mind.

They reached the car. Carson unlocked the doors then climbed behind the wheel. What was she going to say to him? she wondered while he stashed their bags in the trunk.

"You know, Andy has told me so much about you, Carson," Paula said sweetly, slipping into the backseat. "I feel like I've known you for years!"

"Andy?" Carson asked, wondering where that had come from.

"Andy," Paula explained blithely. "Short for Alexander, his name."

"Did the painters come?" Alex wondered as he started to get in the car.

"Oh, sit in back with me, Andy," Paula invited. "Carson will understand! This way you can point out all the local sights."

"There's not much to see at night," Alex told her, but his pride was stinging from seeing Carson with Sam Marshall. He closed the front door and climbed into the backseat with Paula.

Carson waited while "Andy" acceded to Paula's wishes, then she started out of the parking lot. It was going to be a long drive home.

"The painters are finished except for the small bedroom," she said woodenly, refusing to give in to the temptation to look in the rearview mirror at the couple in the backseat.

"How did it turn out?" he questioned.

"I, uh, I didn't look. I've been a little . . . busy."

"So I noticed," he answered. "Sam Marshall."

"Yes," she said in a voice too weak to possibly be her own. She didn't want to go through with the ruse but a look in the rearview mirror at Paula's face changed her mind. She felt like a fool for having thought that Alex might love her.

"That was pretty fast work," he remarked, wanting to ask what she had asked him before he'd left. How serious was it between them? How serious could it be after just a few days? he demanded harshly of himself, not wanting to imagine Carson with the other man. How could she fall for someone who was handsome and well-spoken but obviously a phony?

With a sensitivity born of long acquaintance, Alex listened to Carson ramble on about everything from Rose Creek to a fight in the school cafeteria. She was nervous about something. Or someone. Carson only talked without breathing when she was nervous.

He was exhausted. Five hours in planes and airports. Finding out that Paula had changed her mind about settling down and wanted to marry him. Even if that meant living in Seven Springs. Telling her that it wasn't going to happen between them, that he had changed. Worrying about getting back to Carson again.

"How long have you known Sam Marshall?" he asked finally, interrupting her steady flow of one-woman conversation.

"You sound like an inquisitor, darling," Paula rebuked him. "You aren't her father, you know."

Carson glanced into the mirror, despite herself. Alex had leaned his head back on the seat and his eyes were closed. His voice was strained. Paula looked bored.

But they weren't touching or kissing. In fact, they were sitting on opposite sides of the car. Carson studied them both for a moment, then she looked back in front of her.

"I've met him once or twice before at Melanie's family reunions. Then he came back Thursday for the Rose Creek historical fair."

"And you fell in love with him?"

Carson swallowed hard. "I-I think he's attractive. Don't you? Think he's attractive, that is? I mean, I know he's a man, but—"

"I think he's very attractive, Carson," Paula helped her. "He's tall, well-dressed. Obviously takes care of himself. He looks like he works out. And that was an expensive suit."

"Do you love him, Carson?" Alex wondered, his voice a whisper in the darkness between them.

Carson wanted to cry and spill everything as she had to Lee. Lying to Alex was as hard as she thought it would be, but she shored up her defenses. He was going to marry Paula. Telling him now that she loved him would be like putting her raincoat on under her sweater! The only thing she had left was her pride. Alex would never know what a fool she had been to think of him as anything but a friend.

"Andy," Paula interrupted pointedly, "that's none of your business! The woman has a right to her own life!"

"Sorry," Alex apologized tightly, wishing he had never brought Paula back with him. Wishing he had a few minutes alone with Carson. "I didn't mean to overstep."

What could he possibly say to her now? He should have made it clear before he left. He shouldn't have taken it for granted that she would still be there waiting for him. She couldn't save her heart for him forever.

Carson kept her eyes on the road, wishing they would reach his house. The drive had never seemed so long. She was glad of Paula's presence. The other woman had saved her from breaking down in front of Alex. Her control was only an illusion. She felt like a piece of wet gingerbread.

"I'm sure you're going to love the house," she changed the subject.

"Isn't that wonderful, darling?" Paula helped her move on. "All your hard work has paid off. I can't wait to see Grandma's house. Too bad I didn't bring my red cape!" She laughed at her own joke. Her laugh was like the rest of her, practiced and polished.

Carson felt her stomach turn. She hoped she wasn't going to be sick. She didn't want to think about Paula and Alex in the house together.

"Of course, it'll be good for you to make those finishing touches," Paula continued, oblivious to the heavily charged atmosphere between Alex and Carson. *"Personally."*

Carson took out a tissue and held it to her mouth. If she didn't get out of the car soon, she was going to be sick. There was no power on earth that could save her from looking like a total idiot.

"That's right," Alex answered but didn't sound too pleased by the idea. Resignation hung heavily in his voice. All he could think about was getting out of the car and running to howl at the mountain in despair. What difference did the house make without Carson?

"It'll be good when it's done," Paula explained.

"Since Andy is going to take a bigger role in running the company again."

Carson was astonished. "I thought you wanted to write software and forget that part, An—Alex," she corrected irritably.

"It's a long story, Carson," he replied vaguely, not wanting to talk about anything except her. "So, how serious is this between you and Sam? Do you love him?"

"Andy!"

"It's okay," Carson assured Amy. She certainly didn't need *her* help. "He's really great to be with," she lied expansively. "And he's a lawyer, did you know that? I don't know where he buys his clothes but he always looks good."

"He does dress well," Paula agreed, nudging Alex. "You could learn something from him."

"Do you love Sam Marshall?" Alex tried to pin her down, exasperated with the dance they were doing around the important subject.

"I—"

He sat forward and looked at her. She looked back at him briefly, then focused her eyes on the road.

Paula started to speak, glanced between the two of them, then sat back, not bothering to interfere again.

"I don't know," Carson answered blandly, hurt by his demanding attitude as he sat in the backseat of her car with his beautiful future wife who called him Andy. What did he want from her? She couldn't look at Alex and tell him that she loved someone else, though, when all she wanted to do was tell him that she loved him. She had no pride, it seemed, to protect her from him.

He relaxed at her words. "Carson, have you ever

thought what it might be like if you liked someone as much as you loved him? Someone you knew well. Someone who was like a part of you."

Yes! she wanted to answer but refrained.

"Not really," she replied carefully. "Have you?"

Only for the last year, he thought.

"That's one thing we have going for us, isn't it, Andy?" Paula chirruped. "We're such *good* friends!"

Alex ignored her. He chose his words carefully. He might not have a shot at all with Carson but if there was anything there between them, he knew he had to move in on it quickly. Just the thought of her being with another man made his lungs hurt when he breathed. "I think it would be great to trust someone and enjoy being with them, yet, there would be that intimacy, the closeness of love."

"Melanie's always said that being friends with your husband was a bad idea," Carson quoted. "She and Jake have been married a long time. They seem happy."

"But suppose there could be something more," he enticed her, "something deeper, between two people."

Carson was glad that she didn't have to look at him. The tone in his voice made her want to cry. "I'm glad the two of you are so happy together," she managed to say as she pulled the car into Alex's driveway.

That wasn't what he'd meant, he considered impatiently, wondering then what he had meant and where he was going with all of that. Did he want to tell Carson how he felt about her, despite the fact that she obviously didn't feel the same about him? Just the fact that she had fallen for Sam so quickly made him see that.

"Can you come in for a few minutes?" he asked finally.

"I should go," she answered. "I have to be out at Rose Creek tomorrow before seven."

"Just for a few minutes," he persisted, not wanting to let her go this way. "We could look at the job the painters did on the house."

That was the last thing Carson wanted. A close tête-à-tête with Alex! Her emotions were too raw, too close to the surface. She didn't trust herself to be alone with him in that house that meant so much to both of them.

"Maybe later," she replied quietly. "I have to get home."

"Maybe we can go out with you and your Sam," Paula added. "Wouldn't that be fun? Like double-dating!"

"Are you coming up to Rose Creek for the week-end?" Carson questioned curiously.

"I'm not sure," she ground out, thinking of Sam Marshall. "I have to go out of town again for a few days."

"So soon?" she wondered, trying not to sound as tearful as she felt.

"Andy has to handle this big deal," Paula responded proudly.

Alex frowned, hating the sound of Carson's voice. He knew she was upset but he didn't know why. He wanted to think it was because she loved him and didn't want him to go. He wished that he had a chance to ask her.

"We'll call and set something up, Carson!" Paula waved her out of the drive with the promise after Alex had taken the bags from the trunk.

While Paula showered in the guest room, Alex

stood at the window in his office that overlooked the valley. The moon was reflected in the small ponds that dotted the pasture land. The mountains were black shadows that stood guard on the horizon.

Carson, in her beautiful dress that had made his pulses leap, was on her way home along that silver ribbon of road. When he had seen her face at the airport, he'd thought she was the most beautiful woman he'd ever seen. He hadn't thought about their friendship or anything else . . . until he'd looked up and found another man at her side. That moment had taken twenty years off of his life.

But he knew he was going to see her again before he left. The Historical Society would be expecting him at Rose Creek, and he was going to be there even if it meant gritting his teeth the whole time. The terrible part was that he couldn't even come up with something bad to say about Sam. From what he could recall, he was a good guy, a good football player, and a good friend of Lee's. The last would be a point in his favor since Lee and Carson were close.

When the historical fair was over, he was going to consider selling his grandmother's house. He had imagined his children playing there. His and Carson's children. He might go back to New York. He would probably never see Carson again. He didn't think he could bear to see her walking around Seven Springs with Sam and their children.

Every year, the tiny town of Rose Creek hosted a late fall celebration that included starting up the old mill with its mammoth water-wheel. The county store opened its doors wide to the few thousand tourists that visited and historical societies from around the area joined in by appearing in their finest and demonstrating arts and necessities that had died out in the last two hundred years.

The small battle that had been fought there during the Civil War was commemorated by a similar gathering of people, young and old. They put up tents on the frozen ground and drank from metal canteens as their ancestors had a century before. All of the modern comforts of home were left behind, and they assumed the roles of those stalwart folk.

Cannons were rolled into place around the hillsides that sheltered the little town and fires were built and kept burning while the reenactors chatted with visitors.

Everything was recreated as realistically as possible. No radios or televisions were allowed. Even prerolled cigarettes were banned, and fires had to be started with matches. Outfits were handmade and authentic, for some, down to brass buttons they'd purchased from antique dealers and real army caps.

For the traveling battalions that always stayed together, the order was much more precise and the detail much more accurate. Their officers had earned their ranks and their artifacts had been collected down through the years to be a representation of the real battles that were fought and the way the soldiers had lived on the battlefield.

Carson didn't know how cold it was when the actual battle at Rose Creek took place. She knew that it was freezing that morning. But the weather promised to be warmer later in the day, and the sky was clear, bright blue.

Last year it had been raining, she remembered. She knew she should be grateful.

But she'd lay awake in her bed all night, alternating between hating Alex for coming back, and crying because she was going to be so miserable without him. She'd finally crept from her bed at 4:00 A.M. and made herself a cup of coffee, standing and staring out of the cold, dark window until her mother switched on the kitchen light.

"Is that you, Carsy?"

"I'm afraid so," Carson replied softly, hoping her mother wouldn't notice her red rimmed eyes and splotchy face.

"You're early, even for Rose Creek," she remarked.

"I know. I couldn't sleep."

"Carson," her mother questioned, "are you all right?"

"Fine," Carson answered with a weak smile that threatened to dissolve into tears again. She kissed her mother and ran up the stairs to her room.

She drove to Rose Creek alone, glad to have the time to try to get herself together. She couldn't walk around crying all morning, hoping that no one would notice. She didn't want to have to explain to anyone what had happened between her and Alex.

At least, she consoled herself, she wouldn't have to see Alex. He would be busy with his big project and keeping up with Paula. Unless Carson was mistaken, it was going to take a lot to keep his new bride happy being there in Seven Springs. The closest mall was twenty miles away and the biggest store was Sears.

"Carson!" Melanie hailed her just after she'd arrived at the mill parking lot.

Carson turned and pulled her heavy shawl closer against the cold. Her velvet dress was trailing the frozen ground, a light misting of ice on the dark blue velvet hem. She wore a lace cap on her head that day, her hair coiled up again but not so tightly. Mrs. Engstrom was less exacting away from home.

Melanie stamped her booted feet on the frozen ground and blew into her hands. "I wish they'd have all of these things in the spring and early fall! Why does it have to be either freezing or so hot you can't breathe?"

"I don't know," she admitted. "Maybe we should ask Mrs. Engstrom about that. She makes all the rules."

Melanie looked at her friend closely. "You look ragged this morning."

"Thanks."

"I'm sorry," Melanie apologized at once, dropping the hem of her skirt and following Carson across the frozen ground. "I don't think I've taken this whole thing seriously enough. After seeing the two of you together last night, well, I wish things were different for you."

"Me, too," Carson whispered. Her words turned to mist in the cold. "I'm going to the hospital. I'm supposed to help the doctor today."

"You're lucky!" Melanie frowned. "They've got me riding in an open carriage! In this weather!"

Carson shivered and looked around them at the growing number of reenactors. She didn't want to see Alex, didn't know what she would say to him if he was there. Yet she couldn't help looking for him, hoping she would catch a glimpse of him.

"He's probably here somewhere," Melanie assured her, reading her mind. "Last night, I thought for that one minute that he was upset about seeing you with Sam."

"I don't think Alex is a jealous person," Carson replied quietly. "Even if he didn't have Paula. With her, he probably didn't even notice."

"I know." Even Melanie was daunted by the other woman. "She was gorgeous, wasn't she? How do you think she gets her hair that color?"

"I don't really want to know, Melanie, I—"

She caught sight of Alex, with Sam, no less, across a string of restless horses and smoky fires that several men were trying to coax into warmth. They were talking earnestly between them when Carson nudged Melanie and pointed.

"*Yes!*" Melanie whispered triumphantly. "It's still possible!"

The two men shook hands heartily, and parted with Alex slapping Sam on the back. Sam was in Federal blue that morning. Alex was in Confederate gray. He started walking their way, and Melanie ducked out of sight.

"I'm going to talk to Sam and see what happened," she hissed. "You talk to Alex. Don't give up yet, Carson! She might be gorgeous, but he might love you anyway!"

"Thanks," Carson exclaimed irritably. She'd wanted to see Alex but she'd hoped he wouldn't come that morning. The indecision was killing her.

He almost walked by her. Images of Carson in that slinky little dress still clouded his thoughts that morning, and even when the woman in dark blue velvet cleared her throat as he walked by, he still didn't notice.

"Excuse me, sir," Carson intoned in formal fashion. "Can you loan me some heated socks?"

Alex looked down at her and his eyes widened in surprise. "I've been looking for you!"

She swallowed hard on the sudden obstruction in her throat and blinked back tears that threatened to spill from her eyes.

He took her gloved hands in his and scanned the length of her lightly. "You look great. No corset today?"

"Not today," she replied, trying hard to sound casual. "It's cold, isn't it?"

"Too cold for that shawl," he answered seriously. "Let me find you a coat."

"No, that's okay." She stopped him. "I'm going to be working inside the hospital, so it won't matter. They have a little coal stove in there."

"You're in luck," he told her with a gleam in his eyes. "I'm operating today." He held up the small black bag for her to see.

"How did you—?"

"Alex!" Lee said, advancing on them from behind the wagons. "Good to see you."

"It's been a long time." Alex shook his gloved hand warmly. "I heard that you've been busy in the last few years."

"You know, this and that," Lee acknowledged proudly. "I'd show you their pictures but without having miniature paintings done, that's impossible yet for the average soldier. At least according to Mrs. Engstrom." He shrugged.

"I know," Alex understood his meaning. Black-and-white photographs were around a hundred years before, but color photography hadn't been invented in their current time frame. "Against the rules. Maybe later."

"Agreed." He looked down at his sister. "I think you need to report to the hospital, ma'am. The first bus is already here."

"Can I escort you, ma'am?" Alex volunteered, offering her his arm.

"Thank you," she said graciously. "Where's Paula this morning?"

"She isn't an early riser," Alex explained. "She'll probably be out later. Although she doesn't understand the whole historical thing."

Carson nodded. "I don't blame her." She looked at him closely. "She seems very nice, Alex."

He glanced at her, and their gazes held, clung, then moved away. "She likes you, too."

A crowd had already gathered at the makeshift hospital. They listened to Alex's quickly learned speech about medicine and doctors during the time of the Civil War and earlier.

Carson stood to the side and listened to the sound of his voice, wondering how she had missed loving him when they had been younger. Wondering, after seeing him again, how she would live the rest of her life without him.

"Are you awake, nurse?" he whispered near her ear.

She jumped a little, startled, then turned slightly to gaze into his handsome face. "Yes, sir."

The crowd smiled and speculated when they saw their heads close together, then Alex led them down the rows of neatly stacked cots and away from Carson.

She sat down near the coal stove, ripping material to demonstrate bandaging, glad that there wouldn't be any time for them to talk.

Who would've thought, she considered, that she would be glad that she couldn't talk to Alex? Of course, who would've thought that she would fall in love with Alex?

Alex stood behind her as she was tearing the off-white cotton to make bandages, wondering why he had come. Knowing how hard it would be to see her again. And walk away.

Carson was everything he'd remembered her being. Funny, smart, loyal, ready for anything. It was the rest of her qualities that astounded him. She was beautiful, clever, and strong and he wanted to spend the rest of his life with her.

"Andy?" Paula demanded his attention.

Carson looked back to tell her that he was at the other end of the hospital, and found him, standing over her, his eyes pinned thoughtfully on the back of her head.

"Alex?"

"Carson," he murmured, coming closer to her, "I need to talk to you."

"I came for cappuccino," Paula told them both with a huge, perfect smile. "And I found Sam outside so maybe we can find someplace and get some hot coffee! It's freezing out here!"

There was only one place to get coffee and still stay within the bounds of the historical guidelines. The mess tent was set up near the old grist mill. Paula and Carson sat down on some rough wooden benches while Sam and Alex went for coffee.

"So this is what you do for fun?" Paula wondered, looking around.

"Well, not just this," Carson started to explain.

Paula looked across at her suddenly. "You know, Andy thinks the world of you, Carson. I think you must have been his only friend growing up in this awful place." She shivered in the cold tent and glanced around at the crowd of people gathered there.

"I'm . . . glad," Carson replied carefully. "Alex has always meant the world to me as well."

"But no hanky-panky, huh? Not even a little? All those teenage yearnings and nothing?"

Carson shook her head and smiled. "No one's ever believed it, but its true. There's never been anything like that between us."

"Until now?" Paula demanded coolly.

"What?"

"I've seen the way you look at him, you know? I'm not blind," Paula told her bluntly. "Neither is Alex."

Carson was at a loss for words, wondering frantically what she'd said or done. Or was she so transparent? "I don't know what you mean."

"He knows," Paula whispered as though she was reading her mind. "The way you hang on him, how could he help it?"

Alex and Sam returned with the coffee in metal cups, taking their places beside the two women.

Carson, in a state of shock and panic, afraid that she would give everything away, excused herself almost at once, making up something about helping at the mill.

Alex, seeing her face go very white and hearing the distress in her voice as she fled the tent, excused himself as well, running after her into the cold morning air.

"Well!" Paula exclaimed. "I guess that's the end of that!"

"What?" Sam wondered.

"Probably any hope I had of getting Andy back." She shrugged her elegant shoulders. "So," she wondered with an inquisitive smile, "where *do* you buy your clothes?"

Chapter Ten

Alex followed Carson across the hard, frosty ground that was steaming in the warm sunlight. The back of the blue velvet she wore disappeared into the side door of the old mill behind the huge water wheel. He entered just behind her.

The mill was warm and dimly lit. The sound of the water that powered the milling stones was loud on the ground floor. There was a tour of the mill in progress somewhere above him, but Alex had eyes only for Carson.

"Carson?" he called in little more than a whisper. "Are you okay?"

She didn't look at him, staring straight ahead at the sunlight dancing on the water that was being released for the mill. "Go away, Alex."

He'd heard that tone before. "Is it Sam?"

"No, it's not Sam," she told him flatly.

"Carson," he reminded her. "I know you too well

for that. I know that "I'm all hung up on some guy" voice."

"Really?" she demanded, turning tear stained eyes to him. "Since you know me so well, maybe you can figure out the problem, too."

He closed the distance between them and without thinking, took her in his arms. "I don't care what your friend says about touching you too much."

"You should," she cried, holding her arms tightly to her chest, trying not to touch him. "That's probably what caused all this trouble in the first place."

"Why? Is Sam jealous? Does he think there's something between us?"

"No," she told him honestly. "But Paula thinks there's something between us."

"Paula?" he asked, his heart racing. Had she given him away? Were those tears he saw in her eyes, tears of pity for him? He closed his own eyes, treasuring the few minutes he could stand there with her. Knowing they would have to last him a lifetime. "What did she say?"

"She said she could tell by looking at me that I was in love with you, that I—I wanted to be more than just your friend," she replied, trying not to sob her unhappiness into his shoulder.

"I'm sorry, Carson," he tried to ease her suffering. "She didn't mean it. I know you don't think about me like that."

"You're wrong," she told him, her voice muffled against his uniform. "I don't know when it happened, Alex. But it's true. I—I am in love with you. Lee told me that I should tell you, but I didn't know how. Now, well, I guess it doesn't matter anymore."

Alex held her away from him, looking down into her wet face and red eyes. Without a word, he crushed her mouth under his, his hands holding her tightly against him.

Carson clung to him and wept as she kissed him back with all the passion that she'd hidden from him.

"I think I've wanted to do that almost from the beginning," he told her in a voice that was deep and full of raw emotions. "I love you. You've always been like a beautiful shining angel that made my dark world bright."

He kissed her again, their mouths warm. She trembled as his hands slid up her back.

"I didn't want to live with you as your brother, Carson," he continued, his eyes molten on her face, his hands caressing her back. "I didn't understand then why, but I think I do now."

"You love me?" she asked incredulously, catching that one phrase out of all the rest.

"I love you," he replied, his voice unsteady as he continued to rain kisses on her shoulders and her face. He kissed her mouth again, and she wrapped her arms around him, welcoming the gentle pressure of his lips as he lightly tasted her.

"I was terrified when I came back," he admitted, threading his fingers through her hair. "I'd thought about you so often. I was so worried that you would have changed. Then I got back and you were still Carson, but you were so different. All I've been able to think about is you. And what a mess I'm in!"

"Alex, I—"

"I know this isn't fair." He released her. "I'm sorry, Carson."

She perched carefully on the wide window ledge,

staring at him. "So, that's it? You love me, and you love Paula, and you're caught in the middle? Now what?"

"What about you? You haven't known Sam as long—"

"Sam doesn't mean anything to me!" she told him ruthlessly. "He was Melanie's idea to make you jealous!"

"What?!"

Carson paced the clean cement floor. "I didn't know how you felt about me! I only knew that you were coming back with Paula. Melanie set me up with her brother to make you think about me differently. Or to salvage my pride. Whatever!"

"Carson, you have been corrupted! You're the last person in the world I would've expected to play games like that with me!"

"Games?" she rounded on him. "You want to talk about playing games? What about kissing me as an experiment?" she accused him of the dumb "guy-thing" Melanie had called it.

He frowned. "I was wrong, okay? But I didn't drag someone else into it!"

"You dragged me into it! I didn't want to love you! Why didn't you stay in New York with Paula?"

"Because I wanted to come home," he told her. "Because you were here. Even though I didn't understand how much that meant to me until I left you at the airport two days ago!"

"Is that why you came back with her?" Carson demanded tearfully.

"No," he replied. "She wanted us to get back together. I told her it wasn't going to happen but she said she wanted to come here anyway to see the house. As a *friend,* Carson. That's all!"

Carson swallowed hard, her heart beating rapidly against her chest. "So, you love me and not Paula?"

He nodded. "I'm afraid so. But she does remind me of you."

"Which part?" she questioned, comparing herself to the beautiful, glamorous model and finding no match.

He brought her into his arms again and smiled down into her face. "She kisses a lot like you."

Carson glared at him. "I thought no two people ever kissed alike. Different lip muscles, different size lips, etc., etc.?"

He kissed her lightly. "I meant that she likes to kiss."

"And I like to kiss?"

"You like to kiss *me*," he corrected wickedly.

He put her hands around his neck and drew her closer to him. She complied, waiting until his mouth had almost touched hers then slipped her hand between them.

"What about Paula?" she asked with her hand over his lips. "What will you tell her?"

"I made it plain to her how I feel already," he replied. "If she told you anything else, it was her imagination. Will that do?"

"Nicely," she returned, moving her hand so that she could kiss him.

The mill tour waited patiently for them, then applauded loudly when they had kissed.

"Come on," Alex said, grabbing her hand and pulling her with him out of the mill.

She smiled. "They must have thought it was a soap opera going on right there in the mill for the tour!"

"Since we're both in costume, they'll probably be looking for a historical guidebook to the people who worked the mill!" he agreed with a laugh. "Just like old times, huh, Carson?"

"So, what now?" she asked quietly, her eyes looking directly into his.

"I still have to go back to finalize this deal for Morris. He already knows I won't be staying."

Carson frowned. She knew he was right, but she had waited almost six years for him. She didn't want to wait any longer.

"You could come with me?" he offered, caramel eyes gleaming into hers.

"They could never get a sub teacher that quickly," she replied with a shake of her head. "Besides, I wouldn't want to have anyone else there if you were telling me good-bye."

Alex wrapped his arms around her and kissed her fiercely. "This is the last time I'm going to leave you anywhere, Carson. I'm never going to tell you good-bye again."

"That's good." She sniffed, teary-eyed. "Because I'm never going to let you go again without me. So you better be sure this is what you want."

"You know me better than anyone else on earth, Carson," he claimed. "I want you in my life forever, all your love and your laughter." He touched her cheek with a gentle hand. "And I want to be there in yours. I want to argue with you about who's going to drive and what should be blue, every day for the rest of my life."

He pressed her hand to his lips then kissed her mouth again.

Carson looked at him through a mixture of tears and

laughter and knew that she'd wait. Forever, if she had to, for him.

He left that afternoon in the middle of a snowstorm with Paula waving good-bye to her. Carson had offered to take them to the airport, but Alex had declined.

Sam left with them, not on the same flight, but at the same time. He'd called his lady love and they'd decided to get back together. He credited Carson with the whole thing and kissed her quickly before he boarded the plane.

On pins and needles, Carson waited by her phone, hoping for a call from Alex, telling her when he'd be home. It reminded her of her teenage years when she'd waited for that all important, life or death, phone call.

Alex loved her! She couldn't believe it! After so many years. Despite everything. Alex loved her!

She tried to keep herself from making plans in her mind. Plans that would include their future, their home, their children. Their wonderful life together. She kept the secret to herself, not sharing it with anyone for fear she wouldn't be able to think of anything else.

In her bed, in the warm, dark, quiet of the long night, she had gone over what had occurred in the mill. His kisses had left her stunned and breathless. In just that few moments, she had glimpsed another side to herself that was . . . passionate.

Those happy thoughts occupied her mind through the long hours after he was gone.

Sunday afternoon, he called. She picked up the phone on the first ring, her hand trembling on the receiver.

"Carson?"

"Alex!"

"I'm sorry, Carson—"

"That's okay," she excused rapidly, not caring what it was.

"No, I mean, I have to stay a little longer in the city. Morris had a car accident yesterday. He needs me to step in for a few days."

"Oh."

"Carson? You could fly out here."

She sighed over the promise in the rich texture of his voice. "I couldn't. My class has exams tomorrow. It wouldn't be fair."

"I understand," he replied but disappointment was heavy in his tone.

Carson laughed. "I guess we both grew up, and we're both doing our duty to the establishment."

"I swear I'll drag Morris back to work as quickly as I can, even if I have to threaten to sell the company out from under him."

"I can't wait to talk to you when you get back, Alex."

"I wasn't thinking about the talking part," he suggested, "but that will work, too. I can't wait to get back," he added.

"I feel the same," she answered, feeling a little teary and stilted talking to him on the phone from so far away.

"Promise you'll wear that little dress you wore the other day when I get back?"

She laughed. He *had* noticed! "I promise."

"Promise you won't have that big *GQ* guy hanging all over you?"

"You're the only *GQ* guy I want," she whispered daringly.

"I love you, Carson," he told her in a fierce voice. "I'll see you as soon as I can."

"I love you, Alex. Don't be gone too long, please."

"I won't. 'Bye."

" 'Bye."

Carson went through Monday as though spring had come and lodged in her heart. Alex loved her, and she was secure in her love for him. They would have a wonderful life together in his grandmother's big old house, and hopefully, it wouldn't be long before those grandchildren Martha Langston had wanted so badly were running through the halls and down the stairs.

She sailed through the day on bright wings, not letting anything bother her. Lee stopped in to say goodbye before he left for home. She hugged him tightly.

"Good luck, Carsy," he said, kissing her cheek. "You let me know when the wedding is going to be."

"I will," she promised.

She met Melanie and Jean for dinner and a movie that night. They all picked up their dresses for the reunion that weekend and spent long moments admiring their choices.

"You know, I was on the original prom staff," Melanie told them. "We have the same decorations that we had that night. It's going to be like walking into the past."

"I wouldn't know," Carson replied, smoothing down the heavy folds of her emerald-green satin gown. "I didn't go to the prom."

"You didn't?" the two other women echoed, glancing at each other. "Why?"

Carson shrugged. "I was supposed to go with Alex. He left town before we could go."

"Cheer up!" Jean touched her arm and smiled. "Maybe he'll be back for this one."

"He isn't interested in the reunion," Carson told her. "Too many bad memories for him."

"Well, he's just going to have to get over it," Melanie decided, putting away her own cherry-red dress. "If he's going to live here with you, he's going to have to be a little less the rebel and a little more friendly."

The three women had talked in length about the developments between Carson and Alex, Melanie taking all the credit for the situation.

"Like that stupid thing with Sam had anything to do with it," Jean scoffed.

"It made Alex realize that there was more to think about, didn't it?" Melanie demanded. "He told Carson that he loved her."

"He said he had always loved her." Jean smiled at Carson. "That's different."

Melanie insisted on registering Carson at the three big stores in the mall, saying that she couldn't start preparing for a wedding too soon.

"Alex might not want a big wedding," Carson remarked.

"No one gets married for their own sake," Melanie told her. "You have a lot of friends. We need to have a big wedding for our sake."

"Have you thought about where you might go for the honeymoon?" Jean wondered with a giggle.

"We really haven't even talked about getting married," Carson responded honestly.

Both Melanie and Jean looked at her dubiously.

"You don't think . . ."

"Of course not!" Melanie scorned the very idea.

"What?" Carson wondered.

"Well, he has spent a lot of time in New York," Jean stated.

"What?"

Melanie put her hand on Carson's. "We were just thinking about whether Alex *wants* to marry you. Or if he has something else in mind."

"I don't know," Carson admitted. "I think—"

"Well, we'll just have to come up with another scheme for that, won't we?" Melanie inquired boldly.

"Oh, please!"

"How to get a reluctant man to propose," Melanie entertained the idea for a moment, looking off into the distance for inspiration.

"We don't know yet that he won't," Carson hastened to react after the last fiasco on her behalf. "When he comes back—"

"—we'll see then, won't we?" Melanie smiled slowly like an evil cat.

They went to see a largely forgettable movie and parted afterward, running to their cars through the cold night air.

Carson sprinted upstairs when she reached her house. She had just taken the lovely green gown out of its plastic wrapper when her mother knocked on the door.

"What do you think?" Carson asked when she'd called for her to enter.

Her mother shook her head. "This just gets weirder! Didn't we go out and buy a green dress for the first prom?"

"We did," Carson agreed. "Not anything like this, of course, but I wouldn't have worn this when I was seventeen."

"It is beautiful." Her mother admired the simple but elegant gown. "Try it on for me, Carsy."

The gown was made from a 1940s pattern with a tight waist and long flowing skirt. The neckline was rounded and dipped low across her chest and the back was open to her waist. There were no adornments to take away from the bright color and the richness of the material.

Her mother sighed when Carson twirled around in it for her. "You look like a princess."

"Thanks, Mom."

"Is everything all right, Carson?"

Carson knew when her mother sounded like that, and used her full first name, that she was worried.

"I'm fine, Mom," she admitted. "Better than fine. Alex and I—"

"Oh, no! He's not supposed to take you to the reunion like he was supposed to take you to the prom, is he?"

"No." Carson laughed. "I think we're going to be married, Mom."

"Carson!" Her mother jumped up and hugged her only daughter. "That is so wonderful! You and Alex! After all these years! Your father and I always knew there was something between you."

"So did his grandmother," Carson said, sliding a strand of her hair back behind her ear. "I guess we were the last to know."

"When did he propose?"

Carson smiled awkwardly. "Well—"

"We'll have to get started right away!" Her mother sat back down on the bed. "You know your father's family lives in Alaska. It'll take a while to coordinate that!"

"Well—"

"When are you planning the wedding, Carsy? Even your brothers will need some time to get everything together."

"I don't know yet." Carson consoled herself that it was only a half lie. "When Alex gets back, we'll decide."

"When is he coming back?" her mother asked, a little wariness creeping into her voice.

"In just a few days," Carson replied. "He's supposed to call me tonight."

An exhausted Alex finally did call her about midnight to let her know that things weren't as bad as they had seemed at first.

"I think it might have been a trick to get me to stay out here," he told her. "If I find out that Morris is playing some game with me, I'll choke him."

"I love you, Alex," she mumbled sleepily. "Hurry home."

By Wednesday, everyone was asking her when Alex was due back.

Carson was irritable and impatient from waiting up half the night for him to call her. She'd fallen asleep by the phone a little after 4:00 A.M. with still no word from him, only to rush back out for bus duty at 6:30.

She dragged herself out of her car and up the stairs to her room at the end of the long day. Maybe if she lay down for a little while before dinner, she'd feel more like grading the midterm tests she had stuffed into her briefcase.

She wasn't going to sit by the phone all night again, she reasoned, laying down in her skirt and sweater. If Alex called while she wasn't waiting, he could leave a number, and she could call him back.

She fell asleep almost as soon as her head hit the pillow. It was dark when she awakened, and the rest of the house was quiet.

11:00 P.M.! She looked at her clock on the bedside table and couldn't believe her eyes. She had slept all evening. She yawned and got out of bed, wanting to do nothing more than lay back down and go back to sleep.

There was a message on her door from her mother. Alex had called again, while she was asleep. Her mother had hated to wake her. Alex said he would call back.

The week progressed to its inevitable end, Carson glad that the horrible thing that had started with such promise had finally crawled away.

From her high spirits at the beginning of the week, she had declined to a state of nervous anticipation that included jumping at the sound of every telephone. She couldn't sleep, couldn't eat, and roamed the house fitfully at night.

"You know," her father had joked Thursday night, "if you still had a copy of that terrible song you played until you wore it out the last time Alex left you, I'd be expecting you to play it now."

Carson glared at him, much as the teenage Carson had done five years before, and went to hide in her room.

Saturday dawned bright and clear. Carson had just missed Alex's phone call when she'd run out with her mother to pick up the shoes that went with her dress.

"That settles it," she determined, sitting down hard on the chair beside the phone in the living room. "I'm not moving again until I talk to him." She hadn't spoken with him since Tuesday and had no idea what was going on so many miles away. Was Morris better? When would Alex be coming home?

"I don't understand why he hasn't left a number for you to call," her mother fretted with a glance at her father.

Carson knew what they were thinking. "I know this has been a lot like the last time, but Alex is coming back."

"In ten years or less?" Woods asked, walking into the room.

"Go away!" Carson rejected.

"Woods, please!" his father cautioned.

"No one can take a joke in this family anymore," Woods answered with a shake of his head. "I'm going out."

Carson waited by the phone the rest of the day, but there were only two phone calls. Both of them were for her father.

"Isn't the dance at seven?" her mother asked when her father went out after the last phone call.

Carson blinked as her mother turned on a light in the dark room. "Yes."

"It's nearly six now, Carsy. You might want to get ready."

"I'm not going unless Alex calls," her daughter replied stubbornly.

"Not again, Carson! You have that lovely dress, and all of your friends are expecting you."

Carson smiled slowly. "This is a little too much like it was, isn't it?"

Elizabeth Myszkowski sighed and kissed her daughter's forehead. "Knock them dead, Carsy! You've waited a long time to do it."

Carson shook herself mentally. Her mother was

right. She had waited a long time to go to the prom. She wasn't going to miss it again.

She dressed slowly, hoping against hope that Alex would call. The green dress fell around her like a living jewel, softly rounding her form, lovingly lighting her hazel eyes with green fire.

Her hair was brushed. She had her make up perfect. She stepped into her shoes and pulled on her elbow-length green lace gloves.

"I'm going out," she told her parents as they waited anxiously by the door.

"Have a good time, Carsy," her mother said. "You look wonderful."

"Thanks," Carson replied quietly. "If he calls—"

"I'll tell him," her mother answered, hugging her daughter.

It was after eight by the time Carson arrived at the Whitmore High gym and found a place to park. The stars were bright, and a sliver of moon was visible at the crest of one of the mountains. The lights from the school were glittering, and the sound of the old music was loud in the quiet night.

She wished Alex was there. If he had been there, if he had asked her, she wouldn't have bothered with the reunion that night. She would have been glad to wear the green gown for him.

The far-off drone of a motorcycle engine made her smile as she thought about him and how much he'd meant to her and how much more he meant to her then.

"I love you, Alex Langston," she whispered to the moon and the dark night.

Then she opened the door and the prom came to life around her. Carson looked around her at the subdued lighting and the gold and purple streamers. There were huge fake palm trees and a big yellow moon winking at them from the side wall.

"So, this is what it looked like? This is what I missed?"

Jean laughed. "And you thought it was something special!"

"Hey! We worked hard on this stuff!" Melanie protested. "We—"

"Who's that?" Jean interrupted her friend's tirade.

"He's a little overdressed, isn't he?" Melanie asked, trying to see through the crowd as the promgoers started dancing again.

"Funny how they all wore tuxedos at the real prom," Jean reminisced. "Now, he's the only one."

"That was a long time ago," Melanie told her. "I could barely get Jake to wear a suit for tonight."

The lights dimmed further and a colored spotlight began to dance around the floor with the couples. The music was low and plaintive, a saxophone demanding emotion in the background of the singer's husky voice.

"Where'd he go?" Jean wondered as she looked around the gym.

"He's probably someone's husband," Melanie explained. "No one from Whitmore would—"

"Dance?"

Carson turned slowly, not believing her ears.

"Alex?"

He looked tall and strikingly handsome in his black tuxedo. "I think it's about time, don't you?"

Carson nodded silently and went into his arms.

"You're late," she said when she could speak.

"Better late, my grandma used to say."

"What are you doing here?"

He shrugged. "I told Morris he could either get out of bed and run the business, or it could run itself. He didn't have anything wrong with him, and I wanted to come home. I had a date, you know, even if I am five years late."

"What about Paula?" She wanted to know it all. "Is she all right?"

"Better," Alex informed her. "She's dating Morris. He has a house with three tennis courts and a pool."

"I can't believe you came back."

"I came back for my friend," he replied, his eyes intent on her face as he held her closer.

Carson studied the top of his shoulder, feeling awkward standing there with him, face-to-face with the truth in his beautiful eyes.

"Maybe not so much a friend after all," she murmured.

"Always a friend, Carson." He ran his hand lightly down her gently curved back. "And now . . . so much more."

She looked at him and he bent his dark head and kissed her, the thrill of their touch making both of them shiver.

"Marry me, Carson? Save me from sleeping in that big bed alone?"

She laughed, a tear catching on her eyelash. "Who else is there to save you from all that blue?"

"I'm exhausted," he said, looking at her with evil intent. "Come home and tuck me in?"

She nodded, trusting him as much as she had when they were younger. "I'll get my coat."

When they reached the door, he put his arm loosely around her shoulders. There was a huge black Harley parked at the sidewalk, the chrome gleaming dully in the light from the school.

"Please don't tell me . . . is it yours?" she asked in disbelief.

"Only for tonight," he said with a big smile. "I love you, Carson."

He kissed her and she smiled. "I love you, too, Alex. But I'm not getting on that thing!"

He climbed on and patted the seat behind him. "Shall we hit Mr. Randolph's still on the way home?"

"Only if I'm driving," she said, pushing in front of him on the bike. Her satin skirt slid up her leg.

He wrapped his arms around her and kissed the side of her neck. "Take your time, Carson. I like the view from back here better anyway."